NOTES OF TERROR

NOTES OF TERROR

MARGOT VESEL RISING

iUniverse, Inc.
New York Bloomington

Notes of Terror

iUniverse books may be ordered through booksellers or by contacting:

iUniverse
1663 Liberty Drive
Bloomington, IN 47403
www.iuniverse.com
1-800-Authors (1-800-288-4677)

Because of the dynamic nature of the Internet, any Web addresses or links contained in this book may have changed since publication and may no longer be valid. The views expressed in this work are solely those of the author and do not necessarily reflect the views of the publisher, and the publisher hereby disclaims any responsibility for them.

ISBN: 978-1-4502-6001-5 (sc)
ISBN: 978-1-4502-6002-2 (ebook)

Printed in the United States of America

iUniverse rev. date: 9/21/2010

A special thank you to Mary Thorvig who proof read my manuscript. I would have been lost without her.

Chapter 1

She stood in the hall away from the window that overlooked the town square. It was the eighth of May and flowers were starting to bloom. It should be beautiful this time of year, but she had no wish to look out at the crowd that had gathered in front of the building. She was here for one purpose and only that purpose kept her from fleeing from the too familiar town square. Never in her twenty-eight years had she felt so unsettled.

For anyone who saw her, Laura appeared to be an attractive young woman, tall and straight, her very blond hair flowing neatly to her shoulders. Her ice blue eyes reflected only the nerves she tried not to reveal, nerves that found their way to the surface before each of her concerts. She had learned to live with the butterflies that seemed to flutter in her stomach. That feeling may have been described more as excitement. Either way, it wasn't an unpleasant feeling once she got used to it. It was simply a fact she had learned to deal with. Only tonight, she felt more than the familiar nerves. Flexing her fingers, she looked into space, hoping against hope that she could keep her mind on her music. Still, visions appeared before her, visions of earlier years when she was young and impressionable. Years when she thought she had met Prince Charming and he had come into her life to fulfill her dreams of happiness ever after. How naïve she was, she thought bitterly.

Charles Templeton, an up and coming artist, had wined and dined her. He was culture personified. Laura was mesmerized. Never had she thought she would meet anyone with similar interests. She'd all but given up on any thought of finding a suitable match to her interests and temperament, but there he was. They'd met during her second year of college and she was in seventh heaven. At the end of her third year, he proposed. He wanted to get married right away and wanted her with him when he went to Paris for a year of studying art.

She couldn't believe it. How unfair of him. She never thought that Charles would ask her to give up her studies so he could pursue *his* in Paris. How could he? She asked him to go to Paris alone and they could get married as soon as she graduated. She thought he'd been considering waiting that one year, but she was wrong. She learned from his roommate that he'd left, and without a word to her.

She couldn't believe her ears. She was hurt and the hurt soon turned to anger. She couldn't get over it. He'd left her with a broken heart. She never heard from him again. It took years before she could live a halfway normal life without thinking about him several times a day. Everything seemed to remind her of him, a particular painting or a piece of music. She often saw a man on the street who looked like him, but turned out to be a stranger. Her memories had been so special, it took years to force them from her mind.

An announcement outside jarred her mind to the present long enough to listen to the speaker.

"If everyone will line up in a single row, we'll start letting you into the auditorium. It looks like we'll have people standing in the aisles tonight. Please be patient and we'll move as quickly as possible."

Standing in the aisles? Who was he kidding? The people of Webster City would just as soon run her out of town. Maybe they came to see the intruder who . . . No. She wouldn't bring back those memories. They were too horrible, too hideous to even think of; yet she vividly remembered leaving Webster City that day. She'd been numb with grief, not grief for a man's death, but grief for the withdrawal of the warmth and welcome this city had once bestowed on her.

She couldn't keep herself from turning around and looking down at the swarms of people moving to stand in the single line the ticket-taker had requested. How many people showed up to hear her play? She couldn't imagine this after all those years when her music didn't mean anything to the people of this town. Never had anyone even mentioned it. What possessed them to show up tonight? She imagined that to them, she was a spectacle, someone who had shattered the beliefs of this town. They said that she'd caused a man's death and she let them believe it. Only one man knew the truth.

She paced up and down the hallway of the auditorium. She was nervous now, and she couldn't imagine why because she'd dealt with large crowds many times. She thought she'd conquered her ill feelings for this town a long time ago. Anyway, why should she care what they thought about her now? She didn't feel like a celebrity here. She had composed her pieces and gone on tour for months at a time, playing for audiences from Chicago to Austin, Texas. They were very gracious and treated her like someone truly special. Even the audiences in Europe treated her like a famous celebrity. It embarrassed her, but she guessed it was better than being ignored.

Brad Nielson, a reporter she'd met briefly, came down the hall with a program in his hand. "All set for the big night?" he asked.

"I'm not sure," she answered.

He looked puzzled. "I'd think you'd be on top the world about now."

"Why? Because people who hardly accepted my existence are now willing to listen to my music? I don't think so."

He raised his eyebrow. "You sound bitter."

"Why shouldn't I be?"

"I don't know what you're talking about, but then I've only been here for five years. Is there some history between you and the town?"

She nodded, but had lost some of her belligerence. Perhaps he didn't know about her past. "Quite a history. I'm surprised that you didn't hear all about it when the concert flyers were first sent here."

"And what would they have told me?"

She shook her head. "I really don't want to go into it now."

He nodded. "Of course, but you can't just leave me as confused as I am now. I really need an interview, and I want your autograph on this program," he held it up. "How about getting something to eat after the concert?"

She laughed bitterly. "You mean if they don't run me out of town first?"

He seemed even more puzzled. "That bad, huh? Well, I'll be back stage before you're done and I'll protect you." He flexed his muscles. "I can hold off the best of them if they don't weigh more than a hundred and ten pounds."

She laughed, realizing that it had been weeks since she'd laughed and she felt good about doing it. "Okay, but don't say I didn't warn you."

They were almost seated now. The line was down to about fifteen people. "I'll go into the audience, but I'll see you after the concert. Break a leg or whatever they say."

She watched as he left her standing by the door to the stage. He was muscular and his dark hair graying at the temples and brown eyes made him look friendly. She almost regretted saying what she'd said. She would certainly have to explain after the concert. She heard the PA system screeching and decided it wouldn't be long now. Maybe these were people who didn't know her, who didn't *judge* her because of her talents, but who *appreciated* those talents. She sighed, *Yeah, right! That'll be the day.*

She heard Mayor Wilkins speaking into the microphone. "It is with great pleasure that I welcome a woman well known in the music world. She studied right here in Webster City and is not only a concert pianist having toured the United States as well as Europe, but is a composer known to many, including piano teachers from all over the United States. Please welcome Laura Westlund."

Wearing an elegant burgundy gown, Laura came onstage and sat at the piano. She said a silent prayer that her bitterness would not undermine her ability as a pianist. Moods often influenced the tone, leaving the audience with a completely different interpretation than the original intention of a piece. She told herself to treat this town the same as she had the others and not react in any way to the past. What happened was in the past and she wanted it to stay that way. She could do nothing about it now, not that she would react any differently if she had it to do all over again.

She took a deep breath and entered the world of music that she loved so dearly. Four measures into the piece was all she needed to lose herself in the strains of Chopin. From there, she moved on to Beethoven, Rachmaninoff and Mozart. After almost an hour, she stopped, bowed and left the stage for the fifteen-minute intermission.

She took a sip of water from the thermos she had brought with her and started to pace while the audience relaxed with a glass of wine.

The second half of the program was dedicated to her own music. She wasn't able to cancel this part of the tour, but she could have foregone playing her own compositions here. Her stubbornness dictated the necessity to let these people hear her heartfelt creations. Although she was careful when she named the pieces, she knew that some would feel the emotions she felt when she wrote them. Not everyone, of course, but those who had a true love of music would not only listen to it, but would *experience* it. Some would feel the beauty and peace in *Visions* and *Lullaby*, while they might feel the sadness, the frustration and futility in the others like *Passionata*. Yet others, like *Tempestuous Waters* were written while in mental pain and turmoil but could be misinterpreted as stormy and almost violent. They who listened would hear what they wanted to hear, possibly suggested by the title; but those who *really* listened would feel the joy and elation, or the pain and sorrow, the disappointment and personal loss. That was why she couldn't omit her compositions. If she had to come back to Webster City, she had to be as truthful in her music as she had been in her life, even though she couldn't tell the truth back then . . . except to one man, Craig Thomas. He knew everything and he promised never to tell anyone what really happened that day six years ago.

She was always able to lose herself in her music. She played from the heart and before she knew it, she was standing, taking her bows and accepting the roses that were handed to her. The audience gave her a standing ovation. Tears threatened as she took her final bow, puzzled by the reception. This didn't seem like an audience who blamed her for Fredrick's death.

Finally, the curtain came down and she felt a freedom she hadn't felt in six years. People were lined up to meet her in person. She greeted them and accepted their praise, commenting briefly on how much Webster City had grown. Most of the people were strangers. Toward the end of the line, Police Chief Craig Thomas stood waiting for the others to leave.

"I couldn't make it for the concert. I just got back from Crescent Falls for the last number. It was beautiful." He hesitated, studying her face, "How are you?" he asked with great concern.

"Better than I thought I'd be." Six years had aged him. He must be over fifty now. His dark hair had a good share of gray at his temples and there were deep lines around his eyes and mouth. She supposed that being in law enforcement would have caused them. No matter how quiet a town it was, there was always trouble of one kind or other. Fredrick having been one of the most tragic. She doubted there would have been others as sad.

"I wanted you to know that your presence here was courageous and very well accepted, even needed."

"I doubt that many of them will ever forgive me."

He put his hand on her arm. "I don't understand your thought process. You've done nothing to be forgiven for."

She looked down at the floor. "You know that, and I know that, but this is a city that loved Fredrick for who they thought he was." She shook her head. "I doubt that I would ever be able to change their minds, and I wouldn't try."

He studied her for a minute. "If you feel that way, why did you come back?"

"Frankly, I tried to get out of it, but anything short of being on my deathbed wouldn't satisfy my agent and the powers that be. I'm under contract. I have one more concert next Saturday before I have a few months to myself."

He nodded. "Well, I just wanted you to know. Try to forget what happened then. Many of those people left Webster City and many forgot after a year or so."

"Thank you," she answered, appreciating his concern yet not quite believing him.

He kissed her cheek lightly and turned to leave. "Let me know if you need anything or if you just want to talk."

She nodded before walking slowly to her dressing room and changed from her gown into street clothes. Where had those six years gone?

She remembered the day she first came to Webster City. It was a beautiful city, large enough to support the college, yet small enough to be friendly and involved in community affairs.

Webster City's College of Arts and Music boasted an instructor, a very well-known concert pianist. Fredrick Scofield had toured for more than twenty years all through Europe, Australia and the United States as the most promising young pianist in decades. He suddenly disappeared for a year only to surface at the College of Arts and Music. His arthritis had become so painful and so disabling, that he could no longer play at a professional level.

He spent the year going to clinics all over Europe with no improvement. He came back to the states to the Mayo Clinic in Minnesota, but was told that nothing could bring back the agility his hands needed to continue his tours. Saddened, he settled for sharing his knowledge with young, promising pianists. Laura was ecstatic when she was accepted, and had spent four years in serious study resulting in a contract for one of the most prestigious tours available to artists.

She'd thought that life was wonderful. She was just nineteen when she'd left for Webster City. Life was amazing and she knew she would be rewarded for her many hours of practice and dedication to her music. When she started to compose, it was an outlet for the joy she felt in Webster City. The people were friendly and helpful and she could think of no place she would rather be.

Fredrick Scofield had been delighted with her ability. She sensed his frustration at not being able to play as he had, but he found in her an outlet for his frustration. He would teach her to play as he himself would never play again. Through the years, he became obsessed with her. Unknown to her, he fancied himself in love with her. Even if he was twenty-four years older than Laura, he knew that they both had an unusual and thorough love of music. That made up for the years between them, or so he thought.

"Ready?" asked Brad coming into the dressing room after knocking.

Laura shook off her memories and took her coat from the hanger. Brad helped her into the coat and handed her the purse that was on the end table. "All set?"

She looked around the room and nodded, closing the door behind her.

"You outdid yourself tonight," he said. "You're amazing, but you must know that."

She smiled. "Thank you for saying so. I never get tired of hearing it."

Brad put his hand on her back, and with little pressure guided her to his late model Lincoln.

"Nice car," she commented. "I didn't know they still made Lincolns."

"You'd have preferred a Cadillac?" he teased.

She grinned. "I had you pegged for a Porsche."

He laughed. "A little too rich for my blood and for this town."

"They do have their opinions, don't they." It was not a question, but a pointed statement.

He looked at her, wanting to ask what caused the bitter tone in her voice. Before he had a chance, he was opening the car door for her to help her in. Just as well.

"So how is Webster City treating a big city journalist?" she asked when they were seated at a table near the window.

He shrugged. "I don't know how to answer that. It's a nice city, small enough so everyone is familiar with the next person, but large enough to want what the large cities have. I don't miss New York, if that's what you mean."

"I guess I did. As for wanting what big cities have, to what are you referring?"

"Wealthy people, the best, most creative restaurants and probably the most important aspect, culture."

She'd been studying the menu, but her eyes looked up at him. She nodded. "So that's the reason they wanted the concert tonight?" She sighed. "Nice to know they consider me part of that culture."

"There's that bitterness in your voice again. Care to elaborate?"

She took a deep breath. "It's only fair, but I'd like to enjoy my meal first, if you don't mind." That would give her time to decide just how much she would tell him.

"I don't mind at all. I never did like to do interviews while I'm eating."

"I figured you wouldn't forget about the interview."

Was that disappointment on her face? "If you're thinking that I asked you out for the interview, you're wrong. I wanted to have dinner with you."

"And if I told you I don't do interviews?"

He looked into her eyes trying to decide if she meant what she was saying. "I wouldn't believe you, but I'd have to accept it, wouldn't I?"

"Accepting isn't the same as being okay with it."

"You're right, but disappointed or not, I wouldn't insist. You have as much right to your privacy as anyone else."

She was thoughtful. "Do you really mean that?"

He nodded. "My father was a famous sculptor. He was a private person and wanted nothing to do with the media. He was often downright rude. I understood why, and I understand why you'd like to keep your life to yourself."

"That's nice of you. After we eat, I will tell you some things that you deserve to know, but some of it will be confidential. Can I trust you to keep it off the record?"

"Whatever you say." Just then the waitress came to take their order.

They had a delightful meal, well prepared and beautifully presented. Laura thought back six years and realized that Webster City had evolved into an up and coming community with hopes and dreams that hadn't been apparent when she'd left.

The waitress approached them and asked if they needed anything.

"Please tell the chef," said Laura, "that my walleye was prepared beautifully. In fact, it's the best that I've ever had, and I have been to many cities."

"Aren't you Laura Westlund?" asked the waitress.

She smiled. "Yes. How did you know?"

"Your picture was in the paper. I'll tell Chef Donaldson. He says he knows you."

Laura frowned. "Donaldson?" She shook her head. "I don't remember any Donaldson."

"Well, he remembers you. Let me know if you need anything." She left and went to the kitchen.

Before long, a tall, handsome man in a chef's uniform approached them. "So you don't remember me?"

Laura looked up. "Scotty? Scotty Donaldson," she said as she recognized the man. "But you were an organist and a very good one if I remember correctly."

Scot took a bow. "Still am."

"But a chef, as well?"

He shrugged with a grin. "Some people have more than one great love in their lives. I like to work with food."

"And you do that very well. Scotty, I'd like you to meet Brad Nielson--"

Scot laughed. "Brad's one of my best customers. How are you tonight, Brad?"

"I'm fine. Better than fine. Great prime rib, by the way."

"I'm glad you enjoyed it. Have you ever had anything here that you didn't like?"

Brad shook his head. "Not with you cooking." He turned to Laura. "Scot is the best chef in the area, not that others aren't trying to steal that distinction."

"You're too kind, Brad." He turned back to Laura. "I'm sorry I missed the concert. I had it all planned, but my second in command went to the hospital for emergency surgery this afternoon, so . . ." He shrugged. "Couldn't do anything about it."

"But you own the place, Scot," objected Brad. "Can't you give orders to--"

Scot owned the place? thought Laura.

"I'm responsible for everything here," answered Scot. "Gary was out of the picture and my third in line is in New York at her Uncle's funeral. This couldn't be helped." He watched customers coming in. "I'd better get back to the kitchen. Nice seeing you again. Will you be sticking around for a few days?" he asked as he walked away.

"Not for long. I have another concert on Saturday. Nice seeing you, Scot." She waved as he left. She turned back to Brad. "Now there is a sad story."

"What do you mean? A chef who can cook like that is a *sad* story?"

"No," she sighed, "but he is the most gifted organist I've ever heard."

"As he said, he still is."

"What does that mean?"

Brad laughed. "He still plays the organ at Olivet Church in Hampton Falls."

"That's wonderful, but he's too good to be only a church organist. He could have had his pick of tours. Such a shame."

"I don't see it that way. He's happy, and isn't that what's most important?"

"I don't know. Is it?"

They waited while the waitress cleared the table and refilled their coffee cups.

"Now," said Brad. "Time to spill the beans."

She laughed. "How formal can you get?"

"You said this was off the record. I aim to keep my word. Make sure you tell me what I can print and what follows me to my grave."

She looked into his eyes and determined that he was sincere. She hoped so because she suddenly had a need to talk about what had happened six years ago. Maybe talking about it would allow her to get the monkey off her back. "Where should I start?"

"From the beginning, I guess. I'm in no hurry."

"I was nineteen when I came to Webster City to study with Fredrick Scofield. I assume you've heard of the great concert pianist who had to settle for teaching because of arthritic hands."

He nodded. "He was famous all over Europe, the US and Australia. Such a shame that his arthritis should take that from him, but he still found a way to use his talent."

She sighed. "Yes, but nothing can compare with being onstage, playing for audiences the way no other artist could play. It's fulfilling, truly magical, the greatest reward for a lifetime of work and practice. The realization of his dreams materialized as he pleased audiences made up of all kinds of people. Each one may love a particular kind of music, yet with varying degrees has love for many forms." She hesitated. "It's a feeling that can't be described to know that you've touched each of them in some way."

He watched the light in her eyes as she spoke and knew that she was revealing her own feeling about her music. "A greater love has no man."

"Or woman." She chuckled. "I didn't mean to get carried away."

"It's refreshing to know some people work for reasons other then the almighty dollar. Do you know how few people actually do that?"

She smiled. "If you look hard enough, I'm sure you'll find quite a few."

"That hasn't been my experience, but I look forward to a time that I might actually find the others. I'm honored to meet one right here."

Laura didn't blush often, but she couldn't ignore the heat crawling up her neck and face. She cleared her throat. "What would you like to ask me?"

"I'd like you to finish your story. We got side-tracked."

She nodded. "So we did." She took a deep breath. "It was my last year of study that Fredrick--" She hesitated. "Are you sure this will remain off the record?"

"I give you my word." *It must be something very serious,* he thought. "I hope my word is good enough for you. If not, I could sign a statement."

She smiled and shook her head. "Fredrick started to pay special attention to me during my third year, not that he wasn't always attentive, but he became almost obsessed and uncomfortably possessive. He asked me out to dinner and he took me to concerts. At the time, I thought he was broadening my education, not only exposing me to the world of music, but exposing me to exotic and elegant cuisine that one can't usually find in ordinary restaurants. You know, rounding out my education in all areas." She sighed. "Such a beautiful, wonderful world until," she closed her eyes, her mouth pulled into a harsh line. "Until I realized he was interested in more than my education. It was about a month before graduation that he confessed his love for me. I said nothing. He said he'd wait."

"Wasn't he much older than you?"

She nodded. "Twenty-four years, but that didn't seem to matter to him. Had it been platonic, I could have understood, but one night a week or so before graduation, we were going to the opera. He took me to his apartment where he claimed to have forgotten his wallet. I told him I had money, but he insisted that the tickets were in his wallet." She shrugged. "What could I do? It sounded logical." She shivered. "He took my coat and said we might as well have some tea before leaving. He called me into what I thought was the study, but was actually his bedroom. He had strewn rose petals all over his massive bed." She frowned as if reliving that night. "He took me in his arms and that's when I realized there was nothing platonic about his feelings. I could have forgiven, even understood those feelings, but he wanted more. I tried to stop him, but he became angry and said he had spent four long years cultivating our relationship and that I wasn't going to cheat him out of it." She breathed deeply, "He raped me."

Brad gasped. "You poor kid."

"Well, I was naïve back then, but I learned fast. I told him I was going to the police. He laughed and said nobody would believe me. After all, he had been famous all over the world and could have any woman he wanted. He said many students were more than willing to do whatever he asked, that I should have been happy to accommodate him. I argued, but he said I would not only tarnish my reputation here in Webster City, but it would follow me everywhere the tour took me. Even if a few wanted to believe me, they would always wonder. My agent would no longer want to handle me because my reputation would smear his name as well."

The waitress came to refill their coffee cups. Brad was quiet until she left to refill cups at other tables. "There's more to the story, isn't there?"

Laura lowered her head. "I ran out of his apartment and out onto the street quite hysterical. The Chief of Police, Craig Thomas was driving by when he caught sight of me running. He insisted on taking me to the dorm, but not before he made me tell him what happened. He suggested I go to the hospital so they could check me out. I didn't want to, but he said it was necessary. He said he'd wait for me and take me to the dorm afterwards. I told him what Fredrick had said about my reputation. I didn't want anyone else to know. He spoke to the doctor on duty and was assured it would be confidential. He said it was unfortunate, but what Fredrick had implied was very likely what would happen. The chief wanted to confront him right away, but I said I didn't know what I should do. He suggested that we meet later to talk about it. It was difficult to go through the graduation ceremony with Fredrick sitting up front with the faculty. He had such a smug look on his face. It made me sick."

"Will there be anything else?" asked the waitress whom they hadn't noticed until she spoke.

"No. Everything was wonderful," said Brad, handing her his credit card.

Laura continued. "The chief had attended graduation and insisted on driving me home that night. I could tell he felt sorry for me, no parents to help celebrate; no boyfriend or close friends going to a party. He said we needed to talk, but that we could enjoy ourselves while we discussed the situation. He called his wife and listened intently before hanging up. At his wife's suggestion, he took me to Mason Towers, that beautiful restaurant at the top of the Mason Building. I couldn't have felt less like celebrating, but he made me feel a little more human. We were there until after midnight, hashing over my options."

The waitress placed the check and his card on the table and left.

"To make a long story short, Fredrick was found dead the next day."

"Suicide?"

"That's what they believed, but the police had considered homicide at first."

"How did he die?"

"They said it was an overdose of sleeping pills. He was sprawled on the sofa with an empty bottle of pills on the floor. His arm was hanging downward as if the bottle had fallen out of his hand. Of course, he'd been drinking heavily that night."

"Excuse me for asking, but didn't they consider that you had an excellent motive in wanting him out of the way?"

"Chief Thomas was the only one who knew, and I was with him before, during and after the possible time of death. There was no way I could have been responsible, but people seemed to know that Fredrick's feelings for me were more than those of student and teacher. When I showed disgust every time someone brought up his *infatuation* with me, they assumed that I refused his attentions and that he was heartbroken. Add that to the loss of his playing and they decided it was my fault that he committed suicide."

Brad shook his head. "So you left Webster City."

Laura nodded. "I was under contract to start the tour the following week. I had to leave. But I couldn't have stayed in this town a minute longer."

"So they wrote it up as a suicide and all was forgotten."

She smiled sadly. "That would have been nice, but it wasn't that easy. A couple of reporters got hold of the story and it followed me for the first few months. Whenever I thought it was over, it started again. Suddenly, a reporter would show up and ask for an interview in Chicago, Minneapolis, or any other place. It took almost a year before they dropped it."

Brad shook his head. "How did you manage?"

"I can't tell you how often I wanted to quit the tour and run away to someplace where people didn't know who I was. The only time I felt any sense of freedom was when I was in Europe, and it was probably because I didn't know the language."

"But why did you come back here?"

She frowned. "Ordinarily, I could ask them to skip a city or two, but they refused to cut Webster City. I don't know why. They said it was important that I do the concert here. It's always bothered me. I wish I knew why it was so important."

"As a reporter, maybe I can find out. What are your plans after this?"

She shrugged. "I have a concert in Chicago next week, and then I'm done for a few months. I'm badly in need of a rest." She thought about it. "Could you find out, I mean about the concert here? I would give anything to know. My manager simply told me that his hands were tied. If I wanted to continue the tour for another year, I'd better listen and do what's expected of me."

"That sounds serious. I'll get on it first thing Monday morning."

"Monday?" She was thoughtful. "If I stick around and until Tuesday, do you think you can find out by then?"

"I'll give it my best shot. I can be pretty persuasive when I try to get information out of someone."

She smiled. "I'll bet you can."

He helped her into her coat. "Speaking of information, I have yet to get an interview from you that I can use."

"If it would help, I can give you a couple clippings from other cities. Then you can ask whatever you think is pertinent."

"Good." He drove her to her hotel and interviewed her in the sitting room of her suite. He had as much information as he wanted, or at least that he could use. Nice woman, he thought. Too bad she had to leave. She would be worth pursuing, but as he looked at the baby grand piano in the corner of the room, he realized she was way out of his league. Just as well. He was well over forty and he was too old for her.

"Thank you for everything, Brad. I can't remember a more pleasant interview."

He feigned bruised feelings. "That's all I was to you?"

She laughed. "You're good for me. Thank you for letting me get some of my old feelings off my shoulders. It really helped."

He kissed her on the cheek. "Good night, Laura." He closed the door behind him. As he walked down the hall, the hair on his neck bristled. He looked around, but didn't see anyone. He hadn't felt that way for a while, and when he did, it was something he never took lightly. Something was usually wrong.

He decided to walk down the stairs instead of using the elevator. Halfway down, he turned around and went back up the steps, quietly. He didn't like that feeling and wondered if he was getting paranoid in his old age, even if he wasn't all *that* old.

He stood at the top of the stairs and listened. He didn't hear anything, so he quietly opened the door and slipped into the hallway. As he came to the end of the hall, he looked around the corner and swore he'd seen a shadow moving across Laura's door. It was so fleetingly fast, that he wasn't sure he had actually seen it. Still, he waited there for a few minutes before taking the elevator down. He left feeling very uneasy.

Chapter 2

Laura had the most relaxing day on Sunday. She didn't want to take a chance on seeing people, so she stayed in her room, ordered room service and spent the day practicing and reading a neglected novel. She could get used to this, and she would after her appearance in Chicago.

A pleasant, warm feeling flowed over her as she undressed that evening. She took a shower and washed her hair. When she entered the sitting room, she glanced at the red light flashing on the phone that told her she had a message. She picked up the phone and dialed the desk.

"This is Laura Westlund in room 312. You have a message for me?"

"Yes," answered the desk clerk. "Ellen from the police station asked that you meet with Chief Thomas in his office tomorrow at your convenience."

The food she'd eaten suddenly turned her stomach queasy. "Did she say why?"

"No, Ma'am. You can call her at 222-7655, but I'm not sure she'll still be there."

"Thank you." She hung up and took a deep breath. It didn't have to be anything serious. Maybe he just wanted to tell her if anything was new. New? After six years? She picked up the phone and punched 9 for access and the number Ellen had left for her. She heard it ring.

"Twenty-third precinct. Ellen speaking. May I help you?"

"This is Laura Westlund. You left a message for me?"

"Yes. Will you be able to meet with the chief tomorrow?"

"Did he say what it's about?"

"No. I'm sorry. He was in a rush. He was called out of town. If it's not convenient--"

"No, it's fine. I'll call in the morning."

"That will be fine."

"Thank you. Goodbye." She hung up the phone and sat looking at it as if she could force an answer out of the inanimate object. Why should she be worried? What could have happened in the last six years? Certainly nothing that would make her feel any better than she had then. She still could not understand how Fredrick could take his own life. It was so senseless. At the time, she wanted to believe that someone had killed him, that she had not been responsible for any part of his depression.

She sat down, disgusted with herself. She had been over this millions of times. She'd done nothing to make Fredrick think she had any feeling for him except as her teacher. How could she not know what he was thinking? At the time, she thought he was dramatically over-emotional, as many gifted musicians are. Was she that naïve?

She heard a swishing sound and glanced toward the door. There was a slip of paper that someone had slipped under the door. It was probably the bill for the room. She had told them she would check out on Monday. Many hotels slipped the bill under the door nowadays instead of disturbing those who might still be sleeping. Well, that could wait until morning. She was tired and wanted nothing more than to crawl into bed and get some much needed sleep. This concert was over and she couldn't wait to get out of town. What possessed her to say she'd wait until Tuesday to leave? She knew the answer. It had weighed heavily on her mind that the company wouldn't hear of her canceling Webster City. She sometimes felt that she was not in control of her life. Maybe after another year of tours, she'd be ready to retire and settle down in a nice little cottage in the country, away from cameras and the media; away from people who knew her only as an artist. She longed for friends who wanted to know her as a woman. She wanted a family to replace the parents she'd lost in the fire fifteen years ago.

She slipped under the covers and turned out the light. She could sleep as long as she wanted tomorrow, and she might not get up until noon. Well, maybe a little earlier to call Craig Thomas to let him know she would meet with him. Her last thought was of Craig, how kind he'd been to her. He was like a father to her, more so than her own father. They'd never been close, nor had her mother. She often wondered why they had children if they didn't want a normal family life. Instead, they sent her to the best schools, always far from home while they went gallivanting around the country as free as birds. She was never going to be a parent like that. She sighed. If she didn't get into a relationship soon, she wouldn't have the chance at a family. Her clock was ticking. She laughed. She'd always thought that phrase was over dramatic, but now, it meant something to her. It meant that she had to have children soon, or learn to live without them.

She sighed again. Too bad a woman needed a man to have children; but then, she wouldn't want to raise children without a father. Too bad Charles Templeton turned out to be such a dud. She often dreamed of what life would have been like had they gotten married. She wouldn't have completed her studies, but maybe Fredrick would still be alive. That's what bothered her. Not knowing the truth. Would she ever know? She closed her eyes, and managed to drop off to sleep.

She woke up at nine and called Chief Thomas right away. She agreed to be at his office before eleven. She showered, put on her makeup and got dressed before she remembered the motel bill by the door. She picked it up and briefly looked at it, but it wasn't a bill. She looked again. The sheet of paper was folded in half with her name printed in different colors. Inside, was a message made up of various sizes of words clipped from magazines. She felt faint as she sat on the edge of the bed.

Go Home. You don't belong **here!**
Leave *before* **SOMEONE** gets hurt. Don't make me *say* it **again.**

Laura put the note down and trembled. What could it mean? Who would do such a thing? Suddenly, she wanted to see the chief as soon as possible. She tucked the note in her purse, took her coat out of the closet and left her room.

She drove her rental car to the sheriff's office, parked in front of the building and got out, turned and locked the door. A large mass of dark green caught her attention. She jumped in front of her car and screamed as an SUV almost side-swiped her. It couldn't have missed her by more than two inches. The only thing that saved her was she'd been able to move quickly as she saw it coming straight at her. Evidently the driver didn't want to hit the car and that was lucky. She would have been killed or, at the very least, been crushed between her car and the one in front of hers. She felt weak and wondered if her legs would carry her as far as the office door, but anything was better than staying out here like a sitting duck. That was no accident. But why?

Chief Thomas was filling his coffee cup when the door opened and Laura came in. He noticed the fear in her eyes right away. Her face was as white as the paper on his desk. "Are you all right, Laura?"

She sat in the nearest chair and nodded, not yet able to speak.

"Something happened. What?" He saw her dazed expression.

She started to shake. "I think someone tried to kill me."

He frowned as he sat in the chair next to hers. "Tell me what happened."

She related the incident to him, each sentence ending in a question. "Why would anyone do that? What have I done?"

"Are you sure you're okay?"

She nodded. "Just shaken up."

"As anyone would be." He poured a cup of the fresh coffee and took it to her. "Try this. It might help."

"Thank you." She took a sip. "Why did you want to see me, Craig?" His first name came easily to her. Six years ago, although many years her senior, he had become a very close friend. He was the father figure that Fredrick *should* have been.

"I wanted to call yesterday, hoping you'd stay over a day or two, but a couple of prison escapees had other plans for me."

"Did anyone get hurt?" she asked.

"It was close, but we managed to round them up and get them back where they belong. Took most of the day, though." He cleared his throat. "About why I asked to see you, I wanted to know if you were acquainted with Al Freeman or Carol Harding. Do you recall them?"

Laura looked up as if searching the ceiling for answers. "Carol Harding studied with Fredrick at the same time as I did. As for Al Freeman . . . oh, yes, Alvin did, too. He was . . ." she hesitated, "mediocre at best. As I remember, Alvin Freeman was sweet on Carol, but she didn't return his feelings. Why do you ask?"

He shook his head, "Just a hunch. I've heard a few comments during the years, but something strikes me as abnormal with them. He's still pursuing her and she's warm one minute and cold the next. Sometimes she agrees to see him, but more often rejects him. Actually, it was about a month ago that she went to Flow's Bar and hung one on. She did a little talking that caught my attention. You said she studied under Scofield at the same time as you did?"

"She was very good. She was quite nasty when Fredrick recommended me for the student of the year award. She felt she deserved it more than I did."

"Did she?" he watched her for a reaction.

"I don't know how to answer that. Fredrick often talked about how good she was, but he said that she was too mechanical, too changeable, and far too high-strung. He said she would never amount to anything on the tour circuit."

Craig raised an eyebrow. "High strung?"

She nodded. "She lost her temper a few times, and Fredrick said temper tantrums had no place in music. He was very definite on that." She watched Craig. "What are you thinking?

"Nothing, really. It just seems strange. She made no bones in confessing her undying love for him. She called him Freddie or Fred. She said that you . . . well, to put it kindly, she accused you of manipulating him and monopolizing his . . . affections."

Her eyes opened wide with shock. "And you believed her?" she cried.

He stopped her from saying more by putting his hand on her arm. "I did *not* believe her. It just seems that she was far too bitter for something that happened six years ago. Time heals. People learn to accept truths. Obviously, she wasn't one of them."

"You're thinking that Fredrick didn't commit suicide after all?"

"I have to admit it's still possible."

She took the note out and handed it to him. "I got this last night."

He quickly read it. "You should have called me right away."

"I didn't look at it until this morning. I thought it was a bill that they stuck under my door."

"This makes me more certain that Scofield's death was a homicide."

"But who would want him dead?" She tried to remember the day she was told he was dead. What had she thought then? He'd been drinking heavily. They knew that for a fact. He'd taken a good amount of sleeping pills. "If someone had wanted to kill him," she asked, "how could they have forced him to take the sleeping pills?" She couldn't imagine him doing that against his will.

"I guess that's one of the reasons I almost changed my mind, but it is possible."

"What do you mean *almost*?" She stood up and started to pace the floor. "I thought all along that you were convinced that it was suicide.'

"It was the most logical answer at the time. Who had a motive for wanting him dead, unless . . ." he had just thought of other motives, "unless the famous Fredrick Scofield enjoyed raping women. Suppose there were others."

"For their sakes, I would hope not. For my own sake, I don't know. He was so angry when he told me that he had spent four years cultivating our relationship, it's hard to believe that he would be that angry if he could satisfy himself with other girls."

Craig nodded. "That was my thought at the time. Now, I don't know what to believe, but I'm not happy about your being here with the threat and the attempt on your life. I think you should leave for Chicago right away."

"No," she said stubbornly. "I want to know what's going on. Can't you see, someone wants me out of the way and I want to know why."

"But your safety--"

"Is in my own hands," she finished for him. "Brad Nielson is trying to find out why they wouldn't let me cancel Webster City. Maybe we'll learn a little from that answer. It could have something to do with Fredrick's death. I can't help but think the note does, too."

He shook his head. "I don't like it one bit, Laura. You're the daughter Lydia and I never had. I don't want anything to happen to you and I think you're taking a big chance by sticking around."

"I'm not leaving tomorrow. Please try to understand. I was thinking about sticking around until Friday when I have to be Chicago. I need that extra day to get ready for Saturday's concert."

He shook his head. "We don't have the staff to assign someone to protect you."

"I'll be careful. I promise."

He heard the words, but his mind was already trying to find a way to keep a man watching her for the next few days. If nothing else, he'd take a shift himself. He didn't need more than eight hours off and he knew Lydia would insist on it. That made two men and himself per twenty-four hours. Some city official was going to blow his stack unless he could justify the additional wages, and that wouldn't be easy without revealing Laura's secret. He'd have to think on it.

Laura went back to the hotel. She had managed to convince Craig that they needed to find out why this mess was surfacing again after six years. Maybe what had happened today wasn't connected, but somehow, she felt sure it was.

Shortly before noon, Brad called and asked if she could meet him for lunch. Knowing Craig wouldn't want her running around alone, she suggested that he meet her in the hotel dining room at noon. Meanwhile, she had some serious thinking to do. She tried to recall everything she could about Carol and Alvin. So they were still seeing each other . . . occasionally. Six years is a long time to keep an on/off relationship going. *There must be a reason behind it.*

She went down to the lobby just as Brad approached the dining room. They asked to be seated in a corner away from most of the guests.

After they'd ordered, Laura couldn't wait any longer. "What did you learn?"

"More than I thought." He took out a notebook. "Do you know a Calvin Arneson?"

She shook her head. "No. Should I?"

"I thought you might. He's the nephew of the woman who schedules your tours. Her name is Midge--"

"Midge Mallory," she finished for him. "Of course, I know *her,* but what does her nephew have to do with me?"

Brad smiled. "That's what I'm trying to find out. Stu McGrath is a reporter for the *Chronicle* and a friend of mine."

Laura was thoroughly confused, but she knew he had a point. *Patience* she told herself. "So this Calvin is Midge's nephew."

Brad took a deep breath. "I'll explain it. I connected the dots for you, and what I came up with is that Carol Harding dated Stu, the reporter from the

Chronicle. Stu was a friend of Calvin's. Carol somehow managed to get Stu to ask Calvin to approach his aunt to make certain you didn't skip out on the concert in Webster City." He stopped and let her absorb the information.

"For some reason, Carol wanted me here?" She waited for Brad to nod. "But why?"

"She must have a reason. I've been asking myself that all morning."

Laura's mind flew to the threatening note she received and the attempt to run her down. What connection could there possibly be? "Before you make any more guesses, I should tell you that I received a threatening note at the hotel. Someone stuck it under my door. I thought it was a bill, so I didn't pick it up until morning."

Brad thought back to when he'd seen the shadow on Laura's door. Could that have been when the note was delivered? "When did you first notice the note?"

She thought. "Late Sunday night, I guess. Why?"

He just shook his head, but said nothing. It couldn't have been the shadow he saw. That was Saturday night, but whoever it was could have been trying to determine if she was still in town.

"While we're at it, I should tell you something else." She told him about the SUV trying to run into her.

"My God, Laura! What's going on here? This is getting too dangerous. I think you should go back to Chicago."

"I've already been through this with Chief Thomas. I'll tell you what I told him. I need to find out what's going on here; and maybe what went on six years ago. I have a feeling the incidents are connected."

"I definitely agree, but you shouldn't be foolish enough to think you can take care of yourself when something like this is going on."

She chuckled. "You didn't even give me a chance to say I can take care of myself."

"You were thinking plenty loud."

"Ah. You're really perceptive, aren't you?"

"I like to think reporters are tuned into things that don't penetrate non-journalists. We develop a sort of sixth sense. I suppose we all *have* it, but reporters . . . well, a story often depends on it. You might say we refine that sixth sense."

The waitress delivered their food and refilled their coffee cups. "Will there be anything else?" she asked.

Brad looked at Laura, who shook her head. "We're fine," he answered.

They ate in relative silence, both with thoughts muddling around in their brains. Whoever studied food could make a fortune by designating certain items on the menu as brain food. They sure needed it right now.

Laura ate, but didn't taste anything. Her mind went back to Fredrick. And what was this about Carol? She fancied herself in love with him, yet she dated Alvin and others, if she remembered correctly. Her mind produced a scene in which Carol was trying to seduce Charles. He had painted the picture quite visibly. That's funny, she thought. Charles was an artist. Of course, Charles would relate an incident filled with as much detail as if he were actually painting it. That was the way his mind worked. Why did she suddenly think about Charles Templeton? She'd tried very hard to rid her mind of his memories years ago. They were never really gone, but she kept them below the surface as much as possible.

Brad noticed Laura's eyes on him, yet she was seeing nothing. "What are you thinking about?"

"The past, I guess." But the frown remained and she could feel it. "I was dating an artist six years ago. His name is Charles Templeton. We were engaged."

"What brought him to mind?"

She smiled sadly. "Sometimes it doesn't take much, but I remembered Carol trying to seduce him. He told me about it."

"What happened to him?"

"He wanted me to go to Paris with him where he would spend a year studying under a famous teacher. I felt I needed to finish my last year here to get on the tour circuit. We agreed to pursue our own path for a year and . . . :"

"What happened?"

She shrugged. "Nothing. One minute we'd agreed to wait. He didn't mention it again, but he suddenly left without a word and that was long before he'd intended to leave. I always wondered what happened. Maybe he decided he didn't want to wait, or maybe he was disappointed that I wouldn't give up my studying for him."

"I'm sorry, Laura."

"So am I. He was a wonderful man." She chuckled. "I suppose he still is."

"You never saw him again?"

She shook her head and sighed. "No. Well, you know what they say. Out of sight, out of mind."

"I doubt it where you're involved."

"That's sweet. Thank you." She wanted to change the subject. "What about your romantic interests?"

"Something like yours, I guess. She was a ballerina." His eyes glossed over with a dreamy look. "I had just been hired by the New York Times when her

Ballet company moved to San Francisco. Like you, we each went our own way."

"And where is she now?"

He shrugged. "The last time I heard, they were touring Europe. That was four years ago. For all I know, she's married and has three kids."

The waitress interrupted him. "Do you have room for dessert?"

Laura shook her head. "I couldn't eat another bite."

"Just the check, Phyllis," he said as he looked at her name tag.

She took his credit card and left.

"What are your plans now?" he asked.

"I'll stay for a few more days. I want to know why someone tried to kill me."

"I don't blame you for wanting to know, but I don't like the idea that whoever it was could try again."

"The thing is, the note wanted me to get out of town."

"Okay," he said, watching her.

"Then why did someone try to run me down?"

"Whoever wrote the note last night probably wanted you to leave right away. Yet you were still here this morning." He was thoughtful. "Did you feel like anyone was following you?"

"No. I was too intrigued by how the town has changed, yet stayed the same."

His mind was working silently. "Where were you when this happened?"

"In front of the Chief's office."

He sat up straight. "Now we're getting somewhere. Whoever it was didn't want you to see Chief Thomas. You said it was an SUV?"

She nodded. "A dark metallic green one, you know, as opposed to a flat paint."

"Gotcha. Any license plate number?"

She shook her head. "I was trying too hard to escape injury." She looked down. "I suppose you could have been left half dead and you would have checked the make, model and license plate number of the vehicle."

"We've not only developed our sixth sense, but we've refined our thought process to accommodate our profession." He put his hand on hers. "Don't feel bad. You're a world-famous concert pianist. Why would you need to refine reactions like that?" He shrugged. "We're from two different worlds."

She sighed. "I guess you're right, but I still feel bad that I was too dumb to look."

"Don't waste any energy with that. I need you to dig up memories."

She looked at him, puzzled. "What do you mean?"

"It's a lot like putting together a jigsaw puzzle. You piece bits of information together to come up with facts, or at least, possible facts."

"It almost seems like being given a couple ideas and writing a story from the information." She clasped her hands and rested her mouth on them.

"That's about the size of it. Are you willing to try?"

"What have we got to lose?"

He turned his head to the side, but his eyes never left hers. "Time."

She smiled. "That's fine with me. I'm just biding my time until the concert Saturday. After that, I'm a free woman for a few months."

He studied her. "These tours are pretty hard on you, aren't they?"

"No harder than on any other artist, but you're right. They're exciting at first, but halfway through, it becomes routine and it's exhausting. You stick to the good habits that you managed to perfect. Toward the end, you can't wait to get away from the cities, the stages, the constant practice, the cameras and the media, present company not included. You just want to bury your head in the sand and let life go on without you." She looked down. "At least, that's how I feel. Sometimes I wonder if it's worth it. I guess I'm just plain tired."

He nodded. "That's understandable. And to have this mess to contend with at the same time adds to your wanting to bury your head in the sand."

She nodded. "You're right. Maybe I could accept it more easily at the beginning of a tour."

He laughed. "We could tell them all to hold off for a few months until you're more able to cope."

"What a lovely thought," she said on a sigh. "But let's get real. What would you like me to do? How can I help?"

"Let's plan on a visit to the Library in the morning." When he saw her questioning look, he went on. "I want to see what they have in the archives from six years ago. You said you left right after graduation."

"Yes, as soon as Craig told me I could leave. I should say when he decided to treat it like a suicide. I couldn't have been any help to him after that."

He nodded. "I'll pick you up at ten. Is that too early?"

"Ten is fine. I really caught up on my sleep. Sunday was a lazy-do-nothing day."

He feigned envy. "What does that feel like?" he teased.

"You should try it sometime. It renews you, body and soul."

The waitress brought him the check and his card. She waited while he added the tip and signed the slip. She thanked him and told them to come again.

"He stood and helped Laura up. "Let's fly this coop."

Laura laughed as they walked out together.

Laura slept until eight-thirty Tuesday morning. It had been a pleasant sleep until shortly before she woke up. Her dream involved the SUV coming at her and the fear she'd felt at the time. She looked at the clock and decided it was time to get up if she wanted to go to the Library with Brad. What could he hope to learn there? Certainly, anything that the people involved with Fredrick wanted to keep private, would be something a reporter had no interest in reporting to the public. She frowned. Or would it? She dismissed the thought with the knowledge that she was grasping at straws, and Brad probably was, too.

Brad was there on the dot and they drove to the Library. She stood back while he spoke with the Librarian before they went into a room devoted to old newspapers. She had never seen anything like it. It was impressive.

He told her to sit down while he brought out what he was looking for. He handed her one newspaper while he took the other.

"What am I looking for?" she asked.

"Anything about anyone at the college or about anyone who might have known Scofield."

They were there for almost an hour, having gone through eight papers when Brad suddenly said, "Bingo."

"What did you find?"

He read aloud. "Carol Harding, who studied under Professor Scofield made a statement about his showing preference to a certain prima donna. She states that he told her that she should have received the award that was given to Laura Westlund, an up and coming concert pianist." He skipped to the next paragraph. "Miss Harding stated that she would not confront Miss Westlund. It was enough to know that Scofield preferred her over Miss Westlund." He looked up. "What do you think about that?"

Laura couldn't remember reading that six years ago. "When was it written?"

He told her the date. "Ten days after his death."

She sighed. "That's why I never knew about it." She frowned. "It's strange that she'd say that when Fredrick told me what he thought about Carol's musical ability."

He nodded. "Right. Her temper." He was thoughtful for a minute. "You know, she must have waited until you left Webster City and wouldn't read the local paper. That woman knows how and when to tell a good lie."

He skimmed through several other papers. Finally, Carol was shown in a recent paper. "Look," he said, showing her the paper. "Here's a picture of Carol by her car. It was taken two months ago. Look familiar?"

She shook her head. "Should it?"

"I don't know. It's an SUV."

"Oh," she exclaimed. "Do you think that was the one that tried to kill me?"

He frowned. "I couldn't say, but I wonder if it's dark metallic green."

"Can you find out?" she asked.

"No problem."

Laura looked again. "Why was her picture in the paper?"

"It seems she did a commercial for the dealer." He silently read a few more lines. "She says it's not exactly her field since she is an artist, but it puts food on the table and it describes her as a well-known, talented pianist."

Laura had several questions. "Where does Carol live? Like the rest of us, she was from somewhere else. I assumed that she graduated and moved on out. If she did a commercial, she must live fairly close."

"Not necessarily but you could be right." He took out his notebook, checked something on the picture and jotted it down. "I'll check the license plate number of this car and I'll find out where she lives."

"But the SUV in the picture probably belongs to the dealership."

He shook his head and pointed to the caption below the picture. "It says here that she loves *her* new SUV. They wouldn't advertise that without it being true."

"Okay. So you find out about her. What does that prove?"

"Let's find out what color her SUV is. We'll take it from there. If it's green, I think I'll pay Miss Harding a visit."

"Will you take me with you? I want to look her square in the face and ask her to repeat what she said Fredrick told her about me."

He shook his head stubbornly. "I can sympathize with you, Laura, but I can't let you get involved." She was ready to object, but he stopped her short. "What if *she* was the one who tried to run you down?"

"Well . . ." she didn't know how to answer. She had to admit that it might not be a smart move. "Maybe you should ask Craig to go with you." She noticed the look of distaste in his eyes as she used his first name. She quickly added, "Chief Thomas." She supposed he thought she made it a habit to get involved with older men. "Craig is like a father to me," she explained. "He's the only one who knows what really happened that night. In case I didn't mention it, I was with him from before to after the possible time of Fredrick's death." She looked down. "I was pretty messed up mentally about it. He took me to dinner to get my mind off what happened. I told you that."

"A lot more thoroughly this time. You didn't mention why he took you to dinner."

"Lydia, his wife, had a meeting that night, so he couldn't take me home with him. She suggested he take me to the Towers. I'm so lucky. Just think if I hadn't had an alibi."

"I see your point." He took a deep breath, forcing his attention back to the problem at hand. "So Craig knew about the rape. Are you sure Carol didn't find out somehow?"

"No. How could she?"

He shrugged. "It's a fairly small campus. All it takes is a suspicion and the talk starts. People put two and two together.

"No way! Fredrick lived in a house at the edge of town. There are no neighbors who might have seen us going in."

"Okay. I'll stop in and see the chief. Will he mind?"

"No. I'll call him and tell him why you're there. I'm sure he'll cooperate."

"You do realize that he won't want to be with me when I question Carol."

"Why wouldn't he?" She didn't understand.

"Look, the fact is that I'm asking for details to honor Scofield on the anniversary of his death. My talking to her probably won't suggest that we're bringing Scofield's death into it. If the chief is involved, she'll be suspicious. We don't want her to know what we're thinking."

She frowned. "If you question her, she'll certainly know something is going on." She nodded and sighed. "I understand why you don't want me with you, but--"

"I want you to promise me that you won't go running around on your own. Wait for me or stay here behind a locked door. If you feel the need to leave your room, take a cab to the police station. Keep yourself safe."

She'd been tempted to object, but she saw the sense behind it and she had no wish to go through another experience like that near miss with the SUV. "All right. I promise."

Chapter 3

Laura decided the best way to pass the time was to spend a few hours practicing. She still had to prepare for the concert on Saturday. She wished she were all done with the tour, but going back to Chicago was going *home*. Three years ago, she decided Chicago was the best place to get a condo, so she could have a home base between cities whenever possible. It was nice to have a place to call home, even if she was seldom there. It also gave her a place to rest when she had a week between concerts and it was centrally located in the states. When she was in Minnesota, Wisconsin or Iowa, it wasn't too far to be practical.

It was a nice condo, not too new, but well built. She had her baby grand piano and enough furniture to be comfortable without crowding. She didn't like a room full of knickknacks. She detested dusting and polishing them. Or, maybe she had to spend too much time practicing to allow herself time to find out if she would enjoy keeping them dusted. As it was, she had a cleaning service once a month. If she managed to rent a place in the country this summer, she'd have a chance to find out if she enjoyed housework. She intended to practice as long as was necessary, and that might not be the six to eight hours she often spent at it now. It was time she eased up on that.

By evening, she was pacing the floor trying desperately not to call the cell phone number Brad had given her. He'd said to call anytime if something happened. All she wanted was to know if he'd talked to Carol. Did Craig go with him? She checked her watch and decided to call Craig. That was one way of finding out without showing Brad that she was too curious for her own good. Make that too curious for *his* good.

Ellen answered on the third ring. "Chief Thomas's office. Ellen speaking."

"Ellen. This is Laura Westlund."

"Hi, Laura. What can I do for you?"

"Is the chief in?"

"No," she answered. "He's on a call."

"Do you happen to know if he went with Brad Nielson?"

"No, but even if I did know, I couldn't give out that information."

"Of course. I'm sure he wouldn't have minded, but I'll just wait. It's just so hard to try to pass the time when you're nervous about what might be happening."

Ellen hesitated. "Want to tell me what this is all about?"

"I don't think it's a good idea. I'll just wait. Thank you." She hung up before Ellen could ask any more questions. Craig may trust Ellen implicitly, but she doubted that Ellen was aware of what happened six years ago.

Brad had no trouble finding Carol Harding's address. *Strange*, he thought. *In six years, she'd never been married. That is, unless she kept her own name.* He'd find out soon. The address was not far from where Scofield had lived. He wondered if she'd lived that close six years ago. That was an interesting thought. He pulled up in front of the bungalow, got out of the car and walked up the steps to the front door. "Here goes," he muttered as he rang the doorbell.

The door opened and a red haired woman about Laura's age answered. He assumed it was Carol Harding. "Miss Harding?" he asked.

She narrowed her eyes as she studied him. "Who wants to know?"

Brad laughed, deliberately making her think he was embarrassed. "My name is Brad Nielson. I'm a reporter for the Webster City Courier. I wonder if I could ask you a few questions."

She narrowed her eyes suspiciously. "About what?"

"It's coming close to the sixth anniversary of Fredrick Scofield's death and I want to do an article honoring his life." He smiled shyly. "I guess a lot of people knew him, but I just moved here five years ago and I'm having trouble finding those who stuck around after they graduated."

"Why now, after six years?"

"You don't think he deserved it? He was a world famous pianist before he moved here. People shouldn't forget him just because arthritis made him quit playing concerts."

She thought about it, her eyes always suspicious.

He shrugged. "Well, if not you," he turned to leave, "maybe I can get hold of this Laura what's her name." The minute he'd said Laura's name, Carol stared at him, eyes as cold as ice.

She opened the door wide enough to let him in. "What do you want to know?"

"Anything you can tell me about him. I've read whatever information was written about him in the paper six years ago, but it's not much. I'd like to know what happened to make him settle for teaching at the college after leaving the concert circuit. Anything you can tell, me, I'll appreciate. Nothing's written in stone in cases like this. I'll also appreciate anything you can tell me about his past as a concert pianist if you knew him before. What kind of man was he? What kind of a teacher was he?" He gave her his most sincere, wide-eyed look.

"Sit down." She pointed to the sofa. "Where do I start? Freddie was a great pianist, and it made him a great teacher."

"I understood that you studied with him."

"Yes. In fact, he apologized that he had to give a prestigious award to Laura instead of me. He said he didn't want to, but school politics . . . well, you know."

"Hmmm." He wrote a note in his notebook. "Tell me what kind of man he was. Had he ever been married? Any family? Anything personal you can think of."

"No, I don't believe he was ever married. Freddie would have told me. We were very close. I think, had he lived, he would have proposed to me."

"Really?" he said as innocently as he could. "Then I really came to the right place. What kind of a man was he? I mean, after being so famous, did he carry that . . . you know, holier-than-thou attitude--"

"What are you saying?" she challenged. "Freddie was humble when he was teaching. Whatever he was before," she shook her head, "he didn't act like he owned the world like a lot of people do."

"You mean like other concert pianists?"

"Exactly. Like Laura Westlund. She's smug and arrogant. She probably slept her way up the ladder. Sure she can play, but if you knew her like I did, you wouldn't give her the time of day." She may have tried to sound sincere and truthful, but he couldn't miss the hatred in her eyes. "I'll tell you whatever you want to know. Besides, she's probably long gone by now so it's no use trying to get her opinion. I wouldn't trust it anyway."

You'd believe that especially if you're the one who tried to run her down. "Really? You never can tell, can you. I mean, what someone is *really* like. I've seen it a hundred times."

"Then you know what I mean. Well, let's see, Freddie was a great teacher. We all loved him. He not only knew his stuff, but he was kind and considerate. I never heard him get after students because they couldn't practice, even Laura Westlund. He just worked harder with them. We had other classes that demanded attention, too. He understood that. Of course, he never had any trouble with me. I practiced the piano first before I attended to my other classes. He often said he'd never seen anyone as dedicated as I was." She nodded. "He was something else."

Brad stood up, took a card out of his wallet and handed it to her. "If you think of anything else, call me?"

"Of course." She walked him to the door.

He couldn't wait to get out of there. How that woman thought she could tell stories like that and have people believe her, was beyond him. Are people really that gullible? Was Alvin Freeman that gullible? That brought up another thought. Could he find Al and talk to him? That could be interesting; but first, he had to check in with the chief. He'd promised to share anything he learned. He'd be sure to share not only facts, but the impression he got when she was talking. Carol didn't know that he had a small recorder in his suit pocket. He could get into trouble for not asking for her permission, but he didn't plan to use it for evidence. He wanted the chief to hear the tone of her voice, and could only wish that he'd had a video camera, too. Well, her voice should be enough to convince him that she lied even if he couldn't see her facial expressions, and when she didn't lie she twisted the facts to suit her purpose.

Brad had promised to meet the chief at four that afternoon. They'd agreed on meeting at Craig's office so they could talk freely. When Craig came in carrying two cups of coffee from Starbuck's, Brad was curious.

"I always thought," Brad teased, "that you guys ran on the fuel in those black stained pots you brew."

Craig laughed. "Only in the middle of the night. It's so strong it takes on a life of its own."

Brad laughed.

"What do you have for me?"

Brad took out his notebook. "Carol Harding owns a dark green SUV."

"Ah. I doubt that's a coincidence."

"Oh?' said Brad. He was a little disappointed at his reaction, or lack of it. "Are you planning on arresting her?"

Craig shook his head. "There are probably thirty other people in Webster City who own a dark green SUV. It won't stand up in court. You didn't happen to find out what she was doing when the SUV tried to run Laura down, did you?"

Brad shook his head. "I sure wanted to, but I didn't want to give her a clue that she could be in trouble."

Craig raised his eyebrows. "Good thinking. How did you approach her?"

Brad shrugged. "I said I wanted to do a piece on Scofield to commemorate the anniversary of his death, a tribute to him as a concert pianist as well as a teacher."

"Smart boy. What else did you learn?"

Brad took the recorder out of his pocket, rewound it and laid it on the desk. Carol's voice told her contrived story. When it was finished, Brad shut it off and looked at Craig for his reaction. What he saw was a very angry face and hands drawn into fists.

"I don't get it. What is that woman after? What does she hope to gain by maligning Laura and making herself white as snow?" He looked at Brad. "We both know that she's no angel, right?"

"You bet. I was hoping you could have seen her face when she spoke. An actress, she's not. How does she hope to convince anyone?"

"Look at all the kids trying out for American Idol. Some of them were crushed when they didn't make it because they actually believed they could sing. Don't they know how horrible they sound when they're not talented? It's a mystery to me, but stranger things happen."

"People eat that up. Maybe they like seeing how bad someone can sound." Brad took a deep breath. "Do you know where Alvin Freeman lives?"

Craig thought for a minute. "The friend of Carol's?" Brad nodded.

Craig dug through some files and came up empty handed. He grabbed a telephone book, threw another one to Brad. "Let's check these."

After looking, Brad put his down, but Craig found the name. "Alvin Freeman. 224 Garfield Boulevard, Dalton. It's the next town over."

Brad sighed. "Does it strike you as odd that both Carol and Al have stayed in the area after they graduated?"

He thought about it. "I suppose, but there's no law against it. What are you thinking?"

"I haven't a clue, but it seems strange to me. Most kids come here to get a college education, but leave for greener pastures. What's the attraction here?"

Craig looked at him. "Maybe you should pay him a visit and find out." His head bobbed up and down. "This is pretty neat. You can get answers that I'd never be able to pry out of them, and they don't even suspect our motive. We make a good team."

"When you think about team work, doesn't that imply more than one person?"

Craig grinned. "Yup. Don't sweat it. My part hasn't started yet. I have a few feelers out. We'll compare notes in another day or so. Does Laura still insist on sticking around until Friday?"

"I'm afraid so. I worry about her."

"That makes two of us. Try to persuade her to go on to Chicago."

"I've already tried. She refuses. I can't say I blame her, but I don't like the danger she's putting herself in."

"Well, I'm putting a man on her tomorrow, in fact, around the clock. I've been watching her myself, but there are times when I can't." He sighed. "She's a sitting duck if anyone wants to get to her."

"I warned her about keeping her door locked and not letting anyone in. Still, that's not enough. Sooner or later, she's going to go stir crazy and leave her suite."

"Maybe you'd better keep her with you as much as possible."

"I thought the same thing, but I didn't want to tip our hand with Carol Harding. I'll babysit her tomorrow."

"Good. Maybe she can get something out of Alvin. He was another one of Scofield's students."

He tucked the recorder in his pocket and stood up. "I'll try to keep her occupied for the next two days. After that, she leaves and we can breathe again."

They shook hands, walked out together and went their separate ways to their cars.

Laura jumped when the telephone rang. She'd been jumpy all day, especially because she hadn't heard from Brad.

"Hello," she said, sure it was Brad.

"Miss Westlund, this is Martin Gamble. You probably don't remember me, but we graduated from high school together."

She silently ran through her classmates. "The name is familiar, but I can't place you. What can I do for you?"

"My daughter was at your concert. She was so impressed with your performance that she wondered if you would be retiring to start a school of music of your own."

Taken aback, Laura blinked. "Whatever gave her that idea?" she asked.

"She said that she read that you were taking a few months off to reconsider your future. She was hoping that you'd think teaching would be an excellent choice."

"I believe I was misquoted, but it's nice to hear that someone appreciates me."

"Oh, believe me, it's much more than appreciation. Karen hopes to be a concert pianist. You're her idol."

"How sweet of her. How old is she?"

"Eighteen. She has to accept her scholarship to the College of Arts and Music by the end of the month. She was grasping at straws, hoping she could study with you."

"What a nice compliment." She took a deep breath. "I'm sorry to disappoint her, but I've almost committed myself to another year of tours."

"Who can blame you? I'll give her the bad news. I do thank you for your time."

"You're very welcome. If you'll give me Karen's address, I'll send her an autographed program with a message of encouragement."

"That would make her day." He gave her the address. "It will appease her disappointment a little. Thank you so much."

They hung up. Karen never tired of hearing about youngsters who wanted to follow in her footsteps. It was gratifying.

Again, she waited for Brad's phone call. Realizing that he had no obligation to keep her informed, she tried to make herself think that she had no reason to be angry or irritated. It was even possible that Brad hadn't been able to get hold of Carol.

She went to bed feeling a little neglected, but she had to admit that she shouldn't. Once she fell asleep, she slept comfortably for a while, but found herself dreaming that she was confronting Carol, but speaking gibberish. Analyzing that, she decided that she wasn't sure what she'd say to her. Carol was an unpleasant woman. Even six years ago, Carol did everything she could to make Laura feel inferior, undermining the self-esteem she'd managed to acquire during her years at the College of Arts and Music. Even before her parents died, she felt like an orphan who had no place in the world. It wasn't that they didn't love her, but they were unable to *express* their love for her.

She woke up feeling like she hadn't slept at all. Dragging herself out of bed, she showered and dressed before ordering breakfast from room service. She would rather go down to the coffee shop, but she'd promised to stay in her suite. At first, she objected, but she realized that it was logical.

She'd spent two days practicing for the Chicago concert. It was basically the same composers, but with some variation in selections in case some of this audience also planned to go to Chicago. That happened often, so she didn't want an exact duplication of last Saturday's program. Rodeo performers collected women who followed them from rodeo to rodeo. She thought it was only fitting that the arts have followers, too. Thank God they weren't men who wanted personal favors from her, as well. She liked to think she was more cultured than that. She froze in the middle of her thought. Was she a social snob? She never thought so, but comparing rodeos to concerts—

The phone took her attention, but a sick feeling remained in her stomach. "Hello."

"Laura, it's Craig."

"Hi. Has something happened? Did you learn something new?"

He chuckled. "No. I'm just checking to see if everything is all right. Have you changed your mind about staying?"

"No," she said flatly. "It's just getting a little confining staying here all the time."

"Well, last I heard, Brad plans to spend some time with you. He's been quite a busy beaver."

"That sounds like he learned something."

"Yes and no. Nothing we can use at the moment, but collecting facts usually leads to something more rewarding."

She narrowed her eyes ready to come out with some form of sarcasm, but changed her mind. She was too ready to criticize lately. She guessed that went along with the tension that had been building since she received the threat, not to mention the incident with the SUV. She sighed. "Rome wasn't built in a day, I guess."

"Patience, Laura. We have six years to muddle through. If I interviewed you about six years ago, your memory would be as sharp as a hunting knife, but let's face it; people don't vividly remember things that had little or no meaning for them at the time. Even a week is too long for some people to remember details."

"I suppose you're right." She had to address the other question. "As for leaving sooner, I really don't want to."

"I know that, but if your life is in danger--"

"I'll be fine, but Craig, I do appreciate your concern."

"You know how fond I am of you. I only want what's best for you. You know that."

"What makes you think if someone is after me that they won't follow me to Chicago?"

Craig hesitated. He hadn't thought of that possibility, mostly because whoever was doing the threatening, wanted her out of town. "It doesn't make sense, but it is possible. Okay. You stay, but you have to promise to stay safe. Do as you're told. You mean too much to Lydia and me to--"

"I know. I know. I'll be careful, but you be careful, too."

"Always. Got to run. Be good." He hung up.

Laura was grateful for Craig's friendship. What would she have done without him the night Fredrick . . . She wasn't going there. It always left her bitter and scared. She often wondered if she kept men at a distance because of the rape. More than likely, it was because of Charles Templeton. Sadness overtook her. She didn't want to think about how he'd left her and flown off to Paris never to be heard from again.

She pictured him standing by his easel, painting the sunset behind the chapel, his lovely brown eyes and his hair a shade too long. By now he probably had grown it long and kept it tied back. Who cared? She no longer had feelings for him. At least, that's what she told herself. She didn't date men because she didn't have the time. Starting relationships with men she met on the tour was foolish. Most of the men who'd asked her to dinner were well established in business. A long distance romance was not for her. Maybe Charles felt the same way. Maybe that's why he left so suddenly without looking back. She sighed. Maybe it was for the best.

She couldn't help remembering how sweet he was, how attentive and genuinely concerned he was about her happiness and her music. There wasn't a selfish bone in his body. He knew he wanted to paint, to be a well-known artist. And he was really good. She'd seen articles about him in the papers from time to time. He'd achieved the fame he wanted. People all over the world were aware of his art. He said that people would someday be aware of her music, not only her playing, but her compositions, as well. She sighed. Did he ever consider that without him, it was meaningless? Oh, not that she didn't appreciate fame and fortune. but when they shared their art and success with each other, it was life at its best. Should she have cut her studies short and gone with him to Paris? If she had, the horror and sorrow would never have happened. By the same token, she might not have achieved her status as a world-famous concert pianist.

Six years should have healed her broken heart, but somehow, six years wasn't enough. Maybe in another six years she could look back without the pain. She had to admit that she didn't spend this much thought on Charles every day. Why did she think of him so strongly today? She stood up. She would have to get back to practicing and block out unwanted memories. Work always helped. Is that why she tied herself down to a contract that kept her away from home and a normal life for months at a time? Was she using her talent to keep from thinking about what might have been?

The ringing phone jolted her out of the past. This time she wasn't going to assume it was Brad. "Hello."

"It's Brad. Are you in the middle of something?" he asked.

"Not really. What did you find out?"

"Well, nothing too earthshaking, but I thought we could spend some time together and mull over some of the things. You might have a lot of memories that aren't coming to the surface. We could try to scare up a few of them."

"I'd rather not *scare* them up, but I'll do anything I can to help."

"Has everything been quiet? No more threats under the door?"

She chuckled. "No more . . ." She automatically looked toward the door. "You won't believe this, but there is a slip of paper under the door. It's probably nothing."

"Laura, put the phone down and pick up the paper by the edge. Just in case, touch as little of it as you can. If you have plastic gloves--"

"I have. I always carry them when I travel. Wait a sec." She put the phone down, ran to the bedroom and came back wearing the gloves. As she picked up the paper, she saw the large letters on it. She froze for a moment before she took it back to the phone and read it. "**It is with little doubt that I say you will not see it coming.**" She read. She shivered. "It's in large heavy letters, probably done on a computer. Nothing like the one with the cut out words."

"Hold tight. I'm on my way. I should be there in fifteen minutes." He hung up before she had a chance to say anything else.

True to his word, he knocked on her door fourteen minutes later, not that she had been counting. She opened the door wide so he could enter.

"Got the note?" he asked.

"Hello to you, too."

He half grinned. "Hello, Laura. Got the note?"

She smiled and shook her head thinking *it's no use.* Once he had a question, nothing swayed him from it. She carefully handed him the note.

He nodded. "You're right. It's nothing like the other one." Deep in thought, he rubbed his chin with his thumb and forefinger. "That could be done to throw us off. I'm going to hand this over to the chief."

She just watched as he paced the floor in front of her. "I thought we'd take a drive and see if we can find Al Freeman. What do you think?"

"You're asking me to go along?" she was hopeful, but tried not to sound excited.

He nodded. "You must be ready to get sprung from this joint, huh?"

"Absolutely." She grabbed her jacket and purse and said, "I'm all yours."

If only, he thought. He looked at his watch. "We'll stop by the chief's office first and then grab a bite on the way to see Al. Hungry?"

"I hadn't thought about it, but I guess I am."

"Have you not been eating?"

"Of course," she replied. "It's just that I haven't really tasted what I've eaten. It's been more a matter of survival."

"Bad idea, Laura. Food should be savored and enjoyed. It's one of life's few pleasures. Don't take it for granted."

She chuckled to herself. "If I let myself enjoy and savor every bite, I'm afraid I'd gain a hundred pounds."

"I didn't say you shouldn't be careful, but food is meant to be *experienced.*"

"Sounds like the way I feel about music. I firmly believe that some people listen and absorb, while others experience it. I'm the latter, of course."

He nodded. "I believe you have to have a *relationship* with food, too."

"I have a relationship with my food. It helps me stay alive and healthy, and." she added, "is sometimes enjoyable."

He grinned. "Aha. At least we agree."

He helped her into the car and they talked about his day on the way to the chief's office. She enjoyed being out and seeing the city in which she'd been so happy.

"I'm just going to run in with this threat and I'll be right back. Will you feel safe or do you want to come in with me?"

"I feel quite safe here, Brad. Besides, would someone be following me just to wait until you leave me alone?"

He laughed. "My sentiments, but maybe you *should* come in with me. We can't be too careful."

When they were almost at their destination, Laura pointed up ahead. "You may be able to hand him the note without leaving the car." She pointed to Craig who was just coming out of the building.

Brad beeped the horn to get his attention and pulled up in front of the building. "Open your window, Laura."

Craig approached the car. "Out for a little fresh air?"

"We're going to talk to Alvin Freeman," answered Laura.

"Good. Nice day for a ride. How are you doing, Laura?"

She smiled. "I'm all right. I'll be happy when this whole thing is over."

Craig looked at her skeptically. "You know, of course, there are no guarantees that we'll find enough evidence or witnesses to make any charges."

She shrugged in spite of being more optimistic. "A girl can hope."

He smiled at her. "That she can." He turned his attention to Brad. "Take care of our girl. She's special."

"You bet." He reached over with the note and carefully handed it to him. "She got this today."

Craig took it. "A change of pace, isn't it?"

Brad nodded. "What are you thinking?"

"Oh, I don't know. It's too soon to draw any conclusions. Even observations can be off base at this point. Guess work can shade your way of thinking. We have to keep an open mind, Brad."

"You're right."

Craig looked at Laura, his eyes showing concern. "Go on to Chicago, Laura. Leave today, after your outing, if you must, but get out of town."

She shook her head. "No. I want to see this through."

He just stared at her, trying to decide if there were anything he could say that would convince her to leave. Probably not. He shrugged and stepped back from the car.

Brad waved his hand "We'll be off. See you later."

Laura waved and closed the window as they drove away.

"He's such a nice man." Her tone was warm and friendly.

"He's quite a guy, all right." Brad turned the corner and drove to the freeway.

"Where are we going?" she asked.

"Dalton." He entered the freeway. "That's where Al lives now."

"That's only twenty miles away. Doesn't it seem strange that Carol stayed in the area and Alvin is only a short distance away? I wonder if they're seeing each other."

"According to my sources, it's on again, off again."

She smiled. "Of course. You told me that."

"Yes, I did. Do you have a problem with their relationship? That is, did you have a thing for Al?"

"Me?" She laughed. "Al wasn't my type."

"Why not?"

"Oh, I don't know. He was nice enough, but sort of pushy. He and Carol had the same temperament. Maybe they were meant to be together, but I can see why they'd rub each other the wrong way. They're two of a kind."

"How did Al feel about Scofield?"

"I don't know. There too, he was sort of wishy-washy. One minute he thought the world of him; the next minute he was criticizing him."

"Criticizing him for what?"

She looked up, trying to recall the past. "Many things. He accused him of playing favorites. That, of course, was for my benefit."

"He was competing with you?"

"No. We had different majors. While mine was piano, his was organ, but I had the feeling his opinion was based on Carol's opinion."

Brad nodded. "If she didn't get what she wanted, Al took her side."

"Exactly." A slight frown appeared between her eyebrows. "I was never quite sure what she saw in him, or what he saw in her, for that matter. They didn't seem to be suited to each other, yet she crooked her finger and he willingly went to her. I have a feeling that she only beckoned to him when she wanted him to do something for her."

"She used him and, from what I gathered, he wasn't the only one she used."

"I never have understood why people are like that. Isn't life complicated enough as it is? Mine certainly was."

"It would be interesting to know just how far her relationship with Scofield went."

She shook her head. "I can't believe that, Brad. Fredrick said often enough what a spoiled girl she was."

Brad raised his head and glanced at her. "You never told me that."

"I guess I didn't think of it until just now, but now that I did, I remember it vividly." She smiled. "You know, you're right."

"About what?"

"You told me that we don't talk about things we recall because we don't think they're pertinent. I would never have mentioned it any other time."

"Why not?"

She looked away, embarrassed. "I don't know. Maybe I don't want you to think I'm catty for repeating something like that."

Brad's hand slipped over and briefly covered her hand. "I could never think you're anything but sincere and truthful."

"Thank you," she said and turned her attention to the countryside.

Chapter 4

They arrived in Dalton shortly after eleven. Brad checked the address and drove down the street where Alvin supposedly lived.

"Nice area of town," he commented.

"Alvin must have done well for himself." He checked the numbers on the houses. He came to a duplex and found it to be Al's residence. "Let's go get an interview for Scofield's anniversary article."

As she looked at him, obviously puzzled, he remembered he hadn't told her that it was a good cover. "Oh, well, I told the chief that I'd use the anniversary of Scofield's death as an excuse. I told Carol I want to write an article honoring his life."

"What a lovely thought." Her voice dripped with sarcasm. "If it were anyone else, I'd compliment you on it, but--"

"Don't worry. If I write an article about him, I'll tell the truth, but since you want that part of it to remain undisclosed, I'll respect your wishes."

"Thank you."

"I will, however, mention that there may have been many victims."

"I can't believe that."

"Really? Rape is not a one-time occurrence. It is *not* an act of love or affection, no matter how hard he tried to make it so."

"I guess I knew that, but I don't know if I really accepted it as fact." She took a quick breath. "I mean, he went to such pains to set a romantic scene."

"He might have thought that was the easiest way to have his way with you."

She was silent for a moment. "Maybe."

"Let's talk to Al." He got out of the car and went around to open her door.

When they rang the doorbell, there was no answer.

The door at the neighbor's house opened and a man stepped outside. "If you're looking for Mr. Freeman, he won't be back until next week."

"You don't happen to know where he is, do you?" asked Brad.

"His father took ill. I believe it was someplace in the south, maybe South Carolina and North Carolina. I don't know, but he told me he had to be back by Monday. Is there a message I can give him for you?"

"Not really. I'm writing an article about a former instructor of his. I've been collecting information from as many of his students as I can find. Nothing earth shaking. Just a human interest article. I'll try again if I still need the information. Thanks."

He put his hand on Laura's back and guided her back to the car. She remained silent, for which he was grateful. He didn't want to tip his hand by letting Al know ahead of time that Laura was with him. By next week, she would be long gone, and he could pursue the interview again.

When they were nearly back in Webster City, they stopped at a quaint café for a marvelous meal. They both enjoyed selections from the extensive menu. It was like a suburb of Webster City, but had certainly made it a point to compete with the larger surrounding cities. One might hope to see a menu like this in Chicago or Milwaukee, and since both cities were less than a hundred miles away, it may well have been their motivation.

As they were waiting for their after-dinner coffee, Brad broached the subject of her safety. "Don't you think you should go on to Chicago?"

She looked at him, at first, ready to jump down his throat; but she thought better of it. Craig had said the same thing. Maybe she was being a little stubborn . . . well, maybe more than a little, but she didn't want to be pushed out of the way. Still, since they would not be able to talk to Alvin until next week, she hardly saw the advantage of staying. Unknown to Craig, she had seen evidence that someone was watching her, and since one of the cars belonged to Craig himself, she knew it was his doing. Like clockwork, one car would be with her for eight hours before another one took its place. It might irritate her, but it was sweet of Craig to be so protective, and in spite of everything she'd said, she appreciated it.

Perhaps it was time to leave and get herself ready for her last concert. After that, she could relax. Besides, that way Brad wouldn't have to feel like he had to babysit her. He didn't realize she knew that, too. He was sweet, as well.

Laura packed her suitcase and overnight case. She called the desk and asked them to have her rental car brought around to the front and have someone pick up her luggage and put it into the car. She checked to see that she hadn't forgotten anything. She took a ten dollar bill out of her purse and left it on the dresser for the cleaning woman before she took a deep breath and left the room.

She settled the bill and was on her way to the car when Carol approached her with an unpleasant look on her face. "Leaving so soon?" she snarled.

Laura wasn't sure if she should be annoyed or afraid. She had hoped to avoid the unpleasant woman, but since she hadn't, she wasn't about to be gracious as was her habit. "Is there a reason why I shouldn't?"

Carol was fuming. "It must be nice to do what you want and go where you please. The prima donna must be tired of Webster City."

Laura smiled very slightly, remembering the habit she'd so long ago perfected of killing the enemy with kindness. "My concert is over." Her words were soft and sugar sweet. "Is there a reason I should stay?"

"Only long enough to hear what I have to say."

"And what is that, Carol?"

"That you were responsible for Freddie's death. Don't think I didn't know what was between you. That sweet man was taken in by you, but you had only one purpose, didn't you? To use him to get the award and the contract for the tour. They should have been mine, but you managed to pull the wool over his eyes, didn't you?" Her face was twisted with hatred and envy. She'd been jealous of Laura all along, but Laura never thought it was this intense. "Well, you'll be sorry. A reporter is doing an article on Freddie for the anniversary of his death. I think he'll be interested in knowing all about your tactics and how you left as soon as you had everything you wanted."

"All you would have had to do is work a little harder, Carol. I'm sure if you'd put as much effort into your practice as you did in trying to spoil my chances, you could have made it. You could have what I have, but it was your choice. I had nothing to do with that."

"How dare you." Carol reached out and slapped Laura's face, shocking her so much that she just stood there staring at her. Finally, she turned to leave and Carol grabbed her arm. "Oh, no you don't."

Tom, the desk clerk, witnessed the whole thing and stepped between them. "May I help you to your car, Miss Westlund?"

Laura silently nodded. As he took her to her car, she glanced back and saw Carol standing, stunned. She thanked Tom for intervening. "I don't know what I would have done if you hadn't come between us. She is really angry."

"She's a trouble maker, Miss Westlund. I hope you don't get this kind of reception every place you go."

Laura laughed. "If I did, I think I'd become a waitress or flight attendant." She took a deep breath. "No, people are quite friendly. Carol and I were classmates a few years ago. She's always disliked me."

Tom nodded and he helped her into the car. "She's only one person."

Laura nodded. "You're right. Thank you. This is a nice hotel. I'll tell my friends about it and I think I'll write a letter to your manager. You have gone above and beyond the call of duty." She tucked a twenty dollar bill in his jacket pocket. "Thank you again." She closed the door and drove off.

She needed to stop and say goodbye to Craig. He'd been just as kind to her as he'd been six years ago. She often wondered how different her life might have been if her father had been more like Craig and her mother like Lydia. She would be forever thankful that they had come into her life just when she'd needed a father figure so desperately. She parked in front of the station and went in.

"You win," she said as she stuck her head in his door. "I'm leaving for Chicago."

Craig crossed the room and put his hands on her shoulders. "I can't tell you how relieved I am, and Lydia, too. She's sorry she had to be out of town."

"I'm sorry I missed her, too. Give her my love. I decided that it would be best to go on to Chicago and prepare for my last concert."

He nodded. "Where to after that?"

"I'm not sure. I want to be someplace quiet, away from the city." She smiled. "Maybe I'll just stay in my condo and pretend I'm at some beautiful lake cottage. I haven't decided."

"Well, I wish you the best of luck. Will you leave your phone number so I can keep you up to date, that is, if we learn anything pertinent?"

She reached into her purse, withdrew a card and handed it to him. "The card has my home and cell phone numbers."

"Good enough," he said as he slipped the card into his wallet.

She stood on her toes and kissed him on the cheek. "Thank you for everything now and for six years ago. I can't tell you how much I appreciate you."

"You haven't mentioned that Templeton fellow. Did he ever contact you?"

She looked down and shook her head. Why was it that his name could still remind her of her loss? "No. When he left for Paris," she shrugged, "that was it. I still wonder why he couldn't say goodbye to me, but it was his choice."

"That's too bad. He was a good man."

She nodded and turned to leave the office.

"I'll walk you to your car."

As they left the office, a short, but regal man with an attitude entered the outer office. His hair was turning gray and his pale skin made his face look wiped out. His sharp features seemed to go along with the way he held himself so rigidly. "Laura Westlund," he said in surprise. "How lovely to see you again."

"Professor Standish." She shook the hand he held out to her.

Craig moved forward. "Did you need to see me, Professor?"

"Unfortunately, yes. It is with great trepidation that I must speak to you about my nephew." He turned to Laura. "Eduardo is extremely intelligent. I suppose he takes after me, but he is not only nefarious, but often fulminating." He looked at her with a fond smile. "I remember you as innocuous, very pleasant. You were always able to propitiate a situation." He sighed. "My, how I missed you after you graduated." Not only did he use his well-chosen words to make his point, but his hands flew in every which direction as he spoke. "Eduardo is impossible, irascible, recalcitrant." He sighed, shaking his head. "Enough of my nephew. Tell me about yourself."

Oh, dear. She had hoped to escape a long conversation with the man. "There isn't much to tell. I'm due back in Chicago for another concert."

"I'm sorry I had to miss your concert here, but I was in Ohio for the weekend. It couldn't be helped."

She looked at her watch and at Craig. "Maybe next time. I must run. Nice seeing you again, Professor."

He half bowed. "Nice seeing you, Miss Westlund."

Craig pointed to his door. "Go on in, Professor. I won't be but a minute." He watched as the man did as he was told. He leaned down to Laura as they approached her car. "Tell me, Laura, what did the man say?"

She laughed. "In a nut shell, his nephew is a trouble maker."

Craig shook his head. "All those words to tell me that?"

"His students learned to bring a dictionary to class with them. Who knows? Maybe that was his intention all along. It probably became such a habit, he can't quit."

He kissed Laura briefly on the cheek and stood back as she got behind the wheel. "Take care and stay cautious."

Laura looked into his eyes. "You don't think I'm in danger in Chicago, do you?"

He shrugged. "It can't hurt to be vigilant." He didn't want her looking over her shoulder everyplace she went. That could get on the nerves after a while. "Actually, I thought about it and I think this was a Webster City thing. The threats didn't happen until you came back here. Just be cautious."

"I will." She started the car and waved as she drove off. Craig was one of the few people she missed during the six years since she'd left. He was a prince among men, a very caring man and a good law enforcement officer. No matter what the circumstance, one could always count on Craig to weigh all aspects of any given situation. That was why she was able to tell him about the rape. She knew that he would keep his word and never reveal the secret she'd kept for the last six years. Enough of that, she thought. It was a beautiful day and she was going to enjoy the drive back to Chicago. Just one more concert. She could hardly wait. For some reason, the tour had seemed longer this year.

The Chicago auditorium was packed. She wore an elegant emerald green gown and sat at the piano gracefully. The time flew, her mind totally consumed with her music. The applause was warm and enthusiastic. After the last piece, the applause demanded an encore which she was happy to do. The concert had gone well. There was something appealing about the final concert of the season. She played her heart out mostly because the audience was so receptive. They were wonderful, so wonderful, in fact, that she might even miss the accolades. Of course, there would be a write-up in the paper tomorrow. She always looked forward to that, but it was time she made a decision about her time off. Minnesota had lovely lakes that seemed inviting.

She was headed to her dressing room and had just opened the door when a man's voice called her name. It was not just any voice, but a voice she had not been able to forget for six long years. She turned to see Charles Templeton standing a few feet behind her. The feelings that swept through her were indescribable. Had an electric shock been sent through her body, she couldn't have felt more stunned.

Somewhat awkwardly, Charles hugged her.

"Charles?" she all but whispered as her body went limp in his arms. "What on earth are you doing here?"

"I couldn't come to your concert without seeing you." He moved away from her enough so he could feast his eyes on the woman he'd once loved. Once? No, he'd never stopped loving her. "How have you been?"

His tone was friendly, yet rigid. There wasn't the warmth she'd felt six years ago whenever he'd spoken to her, nor did his eyes have the warmth that used to send her into a tailspin. They were not cold, but definitely guarded. She looked at him like a starving woman would look at a succulent cut of prime rib. He had changed very little. He was slightly heavier, more filled out and attractive than he was when he was younger. His brown hair was shorter than he'd worn it six years ago. The chiseled cheek bones were more pronounced than before. His face had only a few lines by his beautiful brown eyes, lines that might have been caused by laughter. She thought bitterly about how long it took for her laugh to be genuine.

A stage hand interrupted her thoughts. "Miss Westlund, I'll make sure all the flowers get to your dressing room. You've never seen so many flowers."

"Tony," she said as her mind tried to focus on the present, "have them delivered to hospitals and nursing homes. Just save the cards, describe the bouquets and send those to my home. Will that cause you a problem?"

He smiled sweetly. "Not at all. Have a good one, Miss Westlund." He turned to go back to the stage.

"Miss Westlund?" Charles said with surprise. "I would have thought you'd use your married name."

She just stared at him. "If I were married, I might, but--"

Charles frowned. "You're not married? What happened?"

Puzzled, Laura searched his face. "What do you mean, what happened?"

"A few days before I was to leave for Paris, Scofield told me he'd asked you to marry him and that you'd happily accepted. I was beside myself. I couldn't take it so I left Webster City the next day."

She was speechless. "Fredrick said he proposed?" she managed to utter.

"What's wrong with this picture?" he said, aware that something was not right. Was the reason he left based on a lie? Frustration and disbelief were catching up to his depression and jealousy. He'd been bitter for so long, he couldn't absorb the fact that she wasn't married.

Laura's mind went back to six years ago when she learned he had left for Paris. She shook her head. "Are you saying that you left--?"

Charles cut in. "I left because we were engaged to be married. I thought you loved me. You suddenly decided to marry that pompous--" He stopped. "It wasn't so?" he asked slowly, scarcely able to think rationally. "You didn't marry the man?"

She reached out and touched his arm. Now it made sense that he hadn't said goodbye. How could Fredrick have done that, but then, how could he have raped her? All she could do was shake her head. She felt faint. "I have to sit down," she said weakly.

They went into the dressing room and she all but fell into the chair.

All thoughts of embracing her and kissing her vanished when he saw how pale she was. He looked around for water or something for her to drink. He caught sight of a bottle of wine in an ice bucket. He opened it and poured a small amount into a glass. "Drink a little of this."

She shook her head.

"He held the glass closer to her. "It will make you feel better. Your face is as white as the wall behind you."

Dazed, she nodded and took a sip.

"Not as strong as brandy, but better than nothing."

"Thank you." She put the glass down and took a deep breath. "I suppose you think this is funny."

"I'm not laughing, Laura. Tragic, would be more like it. Do you realize what that man cost us?"

Her mind shot through all the arguments they'd had when they discussed their future. Had Charles married and had a family? Most men his age were well on their way to a life they'd worked towards. Somehow, she couldn't ask. Not right now, anyway.

"I'd like to knock some sense into that man." He started to pace as he fisted his hands. "Is he still in Webster City?" he barked.

"Charles," she asked. "You didn't know?"

"Know what?"

"Fredrick was found dead after my graduation."

His eyes opened wide. "Dead?"

She nodded. "They considered it a homicide at first, but couldn't come up with any evidence to support a crime. They wrote it off as suicide." There were too many other facts to bring up right now. "I can't believe you never heard about it."

"In Paris?" He shook his head. "You'd think with his fame, news like that would reach across an ocean, but of course, I wasn't interested in anything that was going on in the world." He recalled what his life had been like at first in Paris. He was going through the motions of living, but felt nothing but bitterness and despair. He'd spent over a year in his studio, painting away all the feelings he was having trouble dealing with. He spent those few daily hours under the tutelage of one of France's most famous artists, an artist, who like himself, had had a love affair with a woman he had lost to another man. *Two of a kind* was what he'd called them.

She was having great difficulty absorbing what he was saying. "But surely when you came back to the states--"

"Laura, I didn't come back to the states until now. I've been in Paris all these years. Why would I come back? The love of my life had betrayed me."

"Oh, Charles." She closed her eyes, and visions of what might have been monopolized her thoughts. She tried to shake them off. Tears gathered in her eyes. All those years, gone.

He had a slight smile. "Your color is coming back. Have you eaten?"

She shook her head. "I usually eat after a concert."

"Good. Let's go to the top of the Hancock Building."

"Just like that?" She snapped her fingers. He'd never get a reservation now.

He smiled. "Just like that." He remembered that about her. She loved to punctuate her words with little movements like making quotation marks in the air with her fingers. How he had missed her! All these years, and he didn't realize just how much until he saw her again. He thought he'd conquered the worst of the pain the last couple years. "You wouldn't deny a starving man a meal, would you?" He took her arm and helped her out of the chair. "Feeling better?"

"Yes, thank you." What had started out as an awkward reunion had turned into a friendly one. She would, however, not give her feelings away. She was happy to see him, but sad that they had wasted six years of their lives.

Fredrick had robbed them of those years, and was responsible for causing her to live alone for the rest of her life. She couldn't look at another man after being with the only man she would ever love. Funny, but until this very moment, she would not have admitted to loving him still. Had she spent six whole years denying what she felt? Yet, there was no hope for them. Surely Charles was not free to pursue her, unless his wife didn't mind his having a mistress, and she would never play that role.

Charles hailed a cab and they rode in awkward silence, each one dreading what he or she might learn if they spoke; yet, speak they must. The cab driver, though efficient enough, gave them a few frightening moments. She would never get used to Chicago cab drivers. Although the ride seemed far too long because of the tension, the cab pulled up to the curb and Charles paid him before getting out and helping Laura out. They went into the building and took the express elevator to the ninety-fifth floor. Laura had been pale from the shock of seeing Charles, but she was twice as white when the elevator seemed to rocket up past the ninetieth floor.

Finally there, they left the elevator and looked in on the filled tables. This time of night seemed to be a popular one for diners. The hostess recognized Laura right away, but what surprised her was when she addressed Charles by name. If he'd been in Paris all these years, how would the woman know who he was?

When they were seated, Charles ordered the wine and the waiter left menus with them. Funny, she thought, but food was the last thing on her mind. She had to find out about Charles, but she was so worried that he was married, she couldn't ask the question.

She hadn't really changed, he thought. He could still read her moods and she had been shocked when she saw him. His first inclination had been to take her in his arms and kiss her. He didn't, however know what to expect from her. Better to talk fist.

Finally, when she found her voice, she spoke. "How did she know your name?"

He looked at her with those teasing eyes. "You are the only one who is recognized the world around?"

"Hardly, but I've been in the states except for a few concerts in Europe." She frowned, troubled by a thought. She was more than a little skeptical. "How is it that you never knew I was there? I was in France once, in London three times, not to mention Germany and Austria. Don't they have newspapers and television there?"

He put his hand over hers. "Had I known you were there, I'm not sure I could have faced you yet. No, I spent those years holed up in my studio, a recluse, licking the wounds which refused to heal."

She couldn't put it off any longer, but she had to gather all the courage she had in order to speak. "Would your wife approve of your being here with me?"

He shrugged and could see that her heart fell at that moment. "Laura, what makes you think I could marry anyone but you?"

She was having trouble putting meaning to his words. She had hoped for so very long, but one day, she knew he'd never come back. Now, he was here. "You never married?" The words came more squeaked than spoken.

He shook his head. "You were my only love." The waiter interrupted as he brought the wine, waited while Charles sampled it and filled their glasses. The waiter took their order. They were silent until he left the table. "Did you think I could love another woman after loving you?"

She just looked at him and realized for the first time the pain he must have experienced during those years. She had experienced pain, too.

He ducked a little so he could look directly into her eyes. He pointed to the wine glasses. "Are these glasses half full or half empty?"

"What?" Her eyes moved to her glass as she shook her head. Stupid! He didn't mean her glass of wine. Before she could speak, he continued.

"Do we look back at all those years and live in the past? Or do we thank God that we found each other again and . . ." His words trailed off.

"You may not want what you see if you know about my past."

He frowned. What could she mean by that? Had something happened? He'd avoid the subject for the time being. They should be someplace more private before going into what could be sordid details of the past six years. He steered the conversation to her tours, where she'd been, how she liked each area. "Did you have time to go sight seeing while you were in France?"

She shook her head. "I saw the Eiffel Tower on the way to the concert hall, but after the concert, I just barely made it to the plane before flying back to the states.

"Well," he said softly, "I think I can show you France with my paintings. They're in an art gallery here."

"In Chicago?"

He nodded. "You know, it's funny, but I don't know why I decided to accept the offer after years of avoiding the states." He turned his head and looked at her, strangely lost in thought. "Do you believe in fate?"

"I think I have to after seeing you again. Is there any other explanation?"

"There's no rhyme or reason for my decision. God is smiling down on us, Laura."

The waiter brought their meals. They were more in a mood to eat and converse amicably. Charles couldn't wait to be alone with her. It had been so long, they had so much to catch up on. How could he have been so stupid when he accepted Scofield's words as truth? Hadn't he known Laura well enough to know she would never marry Scofield when she had been so much in love with him? Self hatred could ruin everything and he wasn't going to let that happen. His thoughts turned to the girl he'd loved with all his heart. He hoped that girl was still here. "They say time heals all wounds. I think ours wouldn't heal because we were destined to see each other again."

She smiled sadly, dreading what he might think after he learned she'd been raped. "Do you think this is a second chance?" She wanted to believe that, but she tried to be logical. Many men viewed a woman who'd been raped as *ruined, damaged goods.* Would Charles?

"Yes." He looked at his almost full plate. "Let's finish our meal. Can we go someplace where we can be alone?"

"I have a condo here."

"You live in Chicago? What ever happened to the small town girl?"

"Chicago is centrally located. I often come back between performances when there's time. Besides, my manager and the woman who schedules my concerts are both here. It's really quite handy."

He nodded and decided his hunger suddenly returned. As they ate, he told her about different places in France, how he used to wish with all his heart that she were there so he could share the experiences with her. That just made him feel worse, so he finally stayed in his studio and seldom left it unless it was to find the scenes he felt were worth painting. "Maybe I had it in my mind all along that someday . . ." He looked down. "I can't believe we're sitting here like this. It's so good to see you. I don't think I'll ever get my fill of that. I must paint you, Laura."

"Do I detect just a tiny French accent?"

He threw up his hands with a smile. "Non importante, mi amore."

Laura laughed. "Charles, isn't that Italian?"

He shrugged and grinned sheepishly. "I told you I seldom spoke with people there. Of course, many tourists approached me while I painted. Americans, Italians or Germans." He shrugged. "Everyone wanted to watch me paint."

She smiled. "I'm excited to see what you've done."

"I hope you have time to go to the gallery with me. When is your next concert?"

"It's yet to be decided. I didn't renew my contract yet."

He studied her. "Are you thinking of quitting?"

She would never have thought of it, but sitting here with Charles, with the man she loved, she couldn't think about playing, about traveling from one place to the next to the next. "I hadn't, but . . ." She took a deep breath. "I have a few months off. If I want, I start the next tour in four or five months. If not . . ." her words trailed off with the thought that she had no idea what she wanted. No, that's not true. She wanted Charles. Did he want her? It was so strange to sit here with him, wanting him to touch her, to hold her, and yet, it was sometimes a little like talking to a stranger. He was the old, familiar Charles, the Charles she'd loved; but there were things about him that were different. Even *she* had changed. How could anyone expect to remain the same after so many years? Life taught you lessons. You learned from them and adjusted to them. Could they find their way back to what they once were?

As if he read her mind, he took her hand in his. "I suggest that we get to know each other again. We have all those years to tell each other about. I'm sure we can't do that in a day, but I know one thing, Laura. I never stopped loving you."

"Oh, Charles." She closed her eyes and thought of the effort it had taken each and every day to try to erase him from her mind. She'd practiced for eight and ten hours a day, keeping her mind focused on the music, but nothing helped. The pain had eased up during the last two years; in fact, she had all but convinced herself that it was for the best, that her life was what God wanted for her. Could she dare hope that she and Charles would be together forever? He was right. They had to fill in all those years that they were apart. After that, there would be plenty of time for the rest of their lives. She suddenly felt relieved, relaxed and . . . happy. She was smiling genuinely for the first time in years.

Charles took care of the bill and they left. He hailed a cab and she gave him the address of her condo. He held her hand all the way to their destination. His eyes didn't leave hers for a second, even during some near collisions as the taxi sped through the city streets. She wanted desperately for him to kiss her, but knew she'd have to be patient. She had yet to tell him about the rape. How would he react?

Chapter 5

It was dark when they entered the building. Even if her condo was in one of the better parts of Chicago, he would be concerned for her safety here. He'd thought of her so often while he was painting, trying to remember her full lips, the softness of her skin, the golden highlights of her blond hair. She was beautiful. He *had* to paint.

She unlocked the security door and they took the elevator up to the tenth floor. Charles watched the numbers light up as they approached each floor. "I hope the elevator never quits on you. That would be quite a climb." *What a dumb remark. Can't you do better?* Would she haul off and sock him if he leaned over and kissed her right now?

She chuckled. "Hasn't happened yet." Her hands shook when she unlocked her door. What would Charles do when he learned the truth? She couldn't help worrying. She'd die if he got angry and left her. No, she wouldn't die. She hadn't died six years ago; but how crushed she would be if she lost him after just finding him. Technically, *he* found her. The idea that she'd even think of that amused her and she shook her head. If she were talking, she'd be babbling. She was doing just that, only silently.

"What a great place," he commented as he looked around. "It suits you." The high ceiling surprised him. In cities, one would expect that it would be an extravagant use of space, but then, one could get almost anything if one had the means. These places didn't come cheap. He was pleased that Laura had done so well with her music.

The living room was large enough to hold a baby grand piano, a couch and three easy chairs, all designed for elegance. The colors were brown and gold. Blue dominated in the dining room. The cabinets that lined two walls were filled with crystal. Everything was gleaming. "You've done well, Laura. I'm glad."

She shrugged. "I found that it didn't mean anything without you. I needed to share my good fortune." She motioned for him to sit down and she took the chair beside him.

He nodded. "I know. I could paint and put everything I had into it, but the finished painting didn't mean anything, not like it did before I left. I always wanted you to see my paintings, to give me your opinion." He looked away. "I missed that most."

"I know." She remembered how hard it had hit her after she'd played her first concert. There was nothing. She felt empty, just as she might well end up feeling if he couldn't accept what had happened to her.

"What's going through your mind, Laura?"

She looked down, knowing she couldn't reveal her thoughts. "I can't believe we're together." She hoped that she sounded convincing. "I feel like I'll wake up and you'll be gone again. I'll be more crushed than ever."

"I won't be far away." He looked at his watch. "I'm not certain I can take the time to delve into the past tonight. I'm sorry, but I have to be at the gallery by eight in the morning. It's past midnight now. Can we get together tomorrow, maybe for lunch?"

"I can fix something here. That way, you can take a cab and come when you're finished at the gallery."

He nodded. "It shouldn't take too long. We need to settle some details for the showing. I hope you'll come."

She smiled. "Of course. I wouldn't miss it."

"So," he said slowly and thoughtfully, "it would be wise to do our talking tomorrow, n'est-ce pas?"

She laughed. "By George, I think you've got it. That was indeed French."

He grinned. "What do you know? I absorbed some of the language after all." His smile faded. "I really think it's best if I leave now."

She made herself nod ever so slightly and took his coat from the closet where she'd hung it. The thought had crossed her mind that if he left, she might never see him again. Logic told her that it wouldn't happen, but since it had happened before, she couldn't completely dismiss it from her mind. She had almost asked if he wanted to stay in her guest room. That was ridiculous since all his things were at the hotel.

As if he read her mind, he took her hand. "Don't look so worried. Scofield isn't around to ruin our plans this time." He looked into her eyes. "I plan to court you, whether it's for a week, a month or a year. We belong together. Tell me you feel the same way."

She took a deep breath. "It's vital that we talk before you commit to anything. You may not like what you hear." She searched his eyes for a reaction, but she knew he had to hear her out first. After that, she'd have to accept whatever happened. She could tell him right now, simply and in few words; but something made her wait. Tomorrow was another day. Seeing him again tonight was too new, too precious to risk losing him right away. If only . . .

Charles put both hands on her shoulders and drew her close. "Until tomorrow?" As he kissed her, he felt her stiffen. It bothered him. He could ask her why she reacted that way, but he knew it wasn't wise. Tomorrow was soon enough. He would see her as soon as he was done at the gallery. "I need a cab."

She nodded and pointed to the telephone. While he called, she walked over to the window and looked down at the traffic below. She wondered if she should suggest that he could stay with her instead of at the hotel. Better to wait and see how things turned out first. She could only pray that he wouldn't think she had encouraged Fredrick in any way. Craig had told her that courts often attributed the rape to the woman leading a man on. Certainly, he'd know she wouldn't do that. Could she be certain?

Charles could tell that Laura was bothered. Her mood was . . . skeptical perhaps? At any rate, something wasn't right, but he couldn't do anything about that tonight. He should have gone right to the hotel and waited to see her tomorrow. Both of them might have gotten some sleep that way. Right now, he doubted that he'd even close his eyes tonight. The meeting at the gallery was crucial to the showing; otherwise, he might have postponed it. He put on his coat and kissed her cheek. "Tomorrow?"

She nodded. "I'll be here."

By mid morning, Laura came to the conclusion that she should have told Charles about her past last night. Nothing was worth the agony she'd gone through. The whole scene back in Webster City came back to her and she knew she had to tell Charles all of it, not just the rape, but the attempt on her life and everything.

She'd shopped for food and went through the motions of making a chicken dish that Charles had been fond of. Had the years changed his tastes? Nerves were getting the best of her. If she got rid of one thought, another took its place. What sane man would want to be involved with a woman with so much . . . garbage? Why hadn't Fredrick chosen Carol over her? Carol was more than willing, she was sure. Didn't she tell Brad that she was sure Fredrick was about to propose? Was there some truth to it? She remembered what Craig had said. Could Fredrick have been intimate with other women? No, not women. *Girls.* They were all so young back then.

The phone rang at eleven. "Hello?"

"Good morning." Charles had a voice that could mesmerize a wild animal. "Still expecting me for lunch?"

"Lunch is practically on the table."

"Hmmm. What are we having?"

She laughed. "You'll find out when you get here."

"If you're going to be that way about it, I'll have to bring wine that goes with anything."

"Oh, all right. We're having chicken."

"Not your Chicken ala Laura?"

She laughed. "I forgot you named it that. I wonder if I've changed it through the years."

"It won't matter. Just being with you . . . well, I don't want to go into that right now or I'll never get there. I'll be there as soon as I can get a cab."

"See you shortly." She hung up and decided she could start the salad.

The phone rang again a few minutes later. "Now what," she said as she picked up the phone. "Hello."

"Laura?" That voice didn't belong to Charles. "This is Craig."

"Hi. Do you have something to report?"

"I want to know how you are. But I do have news of a sort."

"Tell me."

"The desk clerk at the hotel brought me a note that was left under the door of the suite you'd had. He didn't think anything of it when the maid first brought it to him, but after he remembered it had been your suite, he brought it to me. He also remembered having to step between you and a woman who was being difficult. He said she was very angry and that she hit you."

"Yes. That was Carol. I guess I forgot to tell you about it."

"It doesn't pay to keep secrets."

"Spoken like a true father." She took a deep breath. "I'm almost afraid to ask what the note says."

"It says, '*It is with great anticipation that I say you can't hide from me. I will find you.*' He couldn't be sure when it was left there because the suite hasn't been in use since you occupied it."

"That doesn't make sense. Carol wouldn't write that after she talked to me."

"There are two schools of thought on that."

Her intercom buzzed. That meant that Charles was there. "Craig, hold on just a minute." She put the phone down and went to the intercom. "Yes?"

"It's Charles. Want to buzz me in?"

"Come on up." She buzzed the buzzer and opened the door on her way back to the phone. "I'm sorry. I had to let my company in." She wasn't going to say who it was.

"The thing is," she listened as Charles walked into the room and noticed she was on the phone. She motioned him to take off his coat. Craig was still talking. "Brad wasn't able to see Freeman yet. He was hoping that you could be here when he finally does."

"What good would that do? If Alvin won't talk to Brad, he certainly won't talk to me. What are you thinking, Craig?"

"Here's the thing. We know Carol has a dark green SUV. Someone left the first note and told you to get out of town. If she sent the note, she might have wanted to get rid of you before you came to see me. Make sense?"

"Possibly. Do I detect another possibility?"

"Laura, you pointed out that the second note looked nothing like the first one. This one doesn't either."

"You're thinking that someone else wants to kill me?" The words were out and Charles was right beside her before she realized it.

"Someone wants to kill you?" he asked, obviously shocked.

"Your company?" asked Craig.

"Yes."

"All right. We'll talk later. You'd better soften the blow to whoever that was."

She nodded. "Yes. It's Charles."

"Charles Templeton?"

"Yes."

"I'll be darned. Good. I'm glad. Keep in touch."

He'd hung up before she had a chance to say goodbye. She put the phone down and knew she had to explain. He'd stood there looking like he was waiting patiently for her to answer, but the ridges on his jaw line told her he was anything but calm.

"You said we had to talk. Why didn't you tell me last night? What is this all about, Laura. Someone wants to kill you?"

"Originally, I'd thought about eating first, but I guess we'd better get this out of the way."

"I couldn't eat a bite right now."

"Let me check the food and turn down the oven. The chicken can wait a few minutes." She went to the kitchen with Charles at her heels. He put the bottle of wine he'd brought on the counter. It took but a minute to decide the food was fine. "Twenty minutes. It'll be done in twenty minutes."

They went back to the living room and she started her long story. She reminded him about getting the student-of-the-year award. She was chosen the next year for the tour that covered the United States as well as Europe. Fredrick had been responsible for both. "I didn't know that he had other things in mind. You said he told you he proposed?"

"Not only proposed, but that you accepted. Happily."

"Well, he never proposed. I suppose he might have been working up to it." She explained about the rape.

"Oh, my God, Laura." He leaned forward and took her hands in his. "Did you go to the police?"

"No. That is, I told Chief Thomas, but he said I was taking my chances. The victim is often accused of leading the rapist on. Girls throw themselves at their teachers all the time. That made me decide to keep it quiet. Craig took me to the ER, but swore them to secrecy. He made sure they had proof of the rape in case we would want it later. Graduation was difficult, watching his smug face when I was handed my diploma."

"Oh, Laura. I'm so sorry I wasn't here for you. If I had been . . ."

She nodded. "I'm glad you weren't. You would have been Craig's first suspect."

"Did he suspect you?"

"No. Thank God. I was with him that night. He felt sorry for me because I had nobody to celebrate my graduation. He'd thought of taking me home with him, but his wife was working and she suggested he take me to Mason Towers for a late dinner. Fredrick was killed sometime between nine-thirty and one-thirty. I was with Craig until shortly after one."

He shook his head in disgust. "What is this about someone trying to kill you?"

She related the attempt on her life with the green SUV and the threatening notes that were left under her door. "Now, it seems there was another note left under the door of the suite I'd stayed in. Whoever sent it evidently didn't realize that I had left. It's funny. We suspected it was Carol."

He tried to go back six or seven years. "Did I know her?"

She nodded. "She's the one who said Fredrick would have recommended *her* for the student of the year award, but that politics required him to recommend me."

"I remember now. She was a catty girl, a spoiled brat, wasn't she?"

Laura chuckled. "That's what you used to call her."

"You say she has a dark green SUV?"

"Yes, but--"

"Do you think she was the one who left the notes?"

"I don't know. Craig says no. The words on the first note were words cut out of magazines. The others, at least the other two were large heavy words as if they were printed on a computer. Besides, it doesn't make sense if Carol was responsible for all of it. The first note told me to leave town before someone got hurt. Then the SUV tried to run me down in front of the police station. The next note said something like . . let's see," she tried to remember. "Oh, yes. *It is with . . .*something or other *. . . you won't see it coming.* Something like that."

"I'd like to see that note."

"Craig has them. He said the desk clerk gave him one that was left after I'd gone. That one said that I can't hide, that they'd find me." She took a deep breath.

"But it sounds like she or he didn't know you'd left."

"I know. The strange thing is that Carol cornered me when I was on my way out of the hotel. My bags were already in the car."

"She cornered you?"

"She told me off properly. Her face was filled with hatred when she accused me of being responsible for Fredrick's death. She said he'd told her that she should have had my award and that she should have been the one to get the tour contract."

Charles was thoughtful. "How did Scofield die?"

"He was lying on his sofa. Apparently he'd been drinking heavily and had taken too many sleeping pills. The empty pill bottle was on the floor."

"Did anyone think Carol could have done this? I mean given all the information that you've told me, wouldn't she have been a likely suspect?"

"Craig said he'd considered it at one time, especially since Carol tried to implicate me when she was questioned. Unfortunately, the suspicion was dropped when Carol produced an alibi. She'd been with a friend of hers."

He got up and paced the floor. "I need to be here for the showing on Tuesday. After that, what are your plans?"

"I don't know. This whole thing has been so upsetting. Brad wanted--"

He lifted an eyebrow. "Brad? Brad who?"

She smiled at the jealousy in his voice. "He's a reporter who has been trying to get to the bottom of the attempt on my life. He, too, was very interested in what Carol had to say. So far, there hasn't been enough evidence to charge her with it. Craig said that he'd like me there when he interviews Alvin Freeman."

"Who is Alvin Freeman?"

Laura explained Alvin's involvement with Carol. She'd just about had it with bringing out all the upsetting facts, but somehow, she'd felt compelled to tell Charles everything. "That's about it," she said as she stood up, "and if we don't eat now, we'll be throwing charred chicken into the garbage."

"Then, by all means, let's eat." As they walked into the kitchen he took her hand in his. "Let's table this discussion until after lunch. It's better for your digestion."

She agreed. "Do you mind if we eat in the kitchen?"

"I wouldn't have it any other way."

"I just didn't feel like fussing with china and my sterling silver."

They kept their conversation light. Charles told her about incidents that had happened while people gathered to watch him paint. "If I'd been able to see, I would have opted to paint at night when people couldn't watch me." He shrugged. "Still, I got a few sales out of it. Tourists eat up that sort of thing. I often wondered if they knew anything about art, or if they bought my paintings just because they had watched me paint them."

She put her hand on his. "You were always very good. I'm sure they knew what they were buying."

The warmth of her hand seemed to go right through to his heart. The emotion that hit him by her simple touch reminded him of how he'd felt all those years ago. Yes, he'd learned to live without her, but not very graciously. He loved her then and he loved her still. That would never change, not for him. Did she feel the same way?

Laura told him about all the places she had seen while on tour. Most artists were eager to see the various places as tourists on their time off. She seldom left herself time to do much of anything except fall into bed at the end of the day. The next day, she'd travel to the next destination, check out the acoustics, practice a few hours and rest an hour at the hotel before the concert. That schedule seldom varied and it became routine. Day after day was the same unless she had a few days between concerts. At that time, she would fly back to Chicago and stay in her condo until it was time to leave again.

"In a way, Laura, you were doing much the same thing that I was. You, too, became a recluse."

"I guess I did."

"Were there no friends to help you cope in Webster City?"

She sighed. "Only Craig." Charles was right. She hadn't left time to make friends; maybe because she had felt so betrayed by Charles, she wasn't going to risk being hurt again. If they had been so much in love, and Charles could just walk off without a word, a friend could do the same thing. True, friends weren't as close as she and Charles had been, but Laura felt she couldn't deal with any kind of rejection, and decided to live her life in a way that she would avoid any chance of closeness with anyone.

"That was my favorite chicken," said Charles as he folded his napkin and placed it beside his plate.

She grinned. "I know."

"You remembered?"

"Of course. If anyone eats and compliments my food, it's worth remembering."

He sat still, his eyes searching hers. No, it was too soon. He had to take it slowly no matter how fiercely he wanted to take her into his arms. He wanted her with him, to be beside her and not let her out of his sight. He wanted to protect her from all the bad things that were going on in Webster City.

His attention was drawn to a plaque that hung beside the window. "Your award?"

She laughed. "Hardly. This was a plaque given to me by the Webster Nursing Home. I went there once a month and played for them. They were so thankful that they presented me with that plaque." She blushed. "I hung it there to remind me of them. Next to practicing, I spend most of my time in the kitchen."

"You always did like to cook."

She laughed again. "Once I got the hang of it. I was a slow starter. I had no mother to teach me how." She looked down sadly.

"I shouldn't have brought it up. I'm sorry."

"Don't be. I've learned to live with it. I believe I had learned that way back when we were in college together."

"I thought you had, but maybe what happened now made the past seem so much more tragic to you."

"You know, the most tragic is the feeling that they didn't care. I was no more than an interruption keeping them from their happy-go-lucky life. It wasn't until they sent me away to boarding school that they could resume the life they'd chosen."

"And then you thought I betrayed you, so all those feelings came back."

She couldn't lie about it. "I suppose."

"Look. I have to be here on Tuesday. Let's go back to Webster City on Wednesday and see what we can find out. You can't go on fearing for your life, Laura. I'm here now, and I'll do everything I can to protect you and to help in any way I can to find out the truth." He watched her eyes as thoughts sped through her mind. "I promise. I won't leave you again. We'll take it slowly, get reacquainted, but after that I want to start over or at least, go on from where we were before I left. He watched her eyes moving from one corner of the room to the other. She was avoiding answering. He knew she was gun shy, and he couldn't blame her, but he had to get his point across. "I love you and I want you in my life. We've wasted too many years. Can you learn to trust me again?"

If only he knew how much she wanted to, but. knowing what she now knew, it wasn't Charles she couldn't trust. It was . . . fate? "What good will it do to go to Webster City?"

For one thing, he thought, it would remind her of how much they loved each other then. "We'll talk to Brad and Craig and try to come to some conclusions." He lifted her chin with his finger. "What do you say?"

She wasn't sure, but she wanted to try. She nodded.

"All right. The first thing we'll do is reserve the suite you stayed in before. What did you have? A bedroom, bath and sitting room?"

"And a small kitchenette."

"Perfect. Did the sitting room have a fold out couch?" She nodded. "Then we'll reserve just a room for me close by, but I will be staying with you in the suite. I'll use the fold out couch." She looked puzzled. "It's for a good reason. I will not leave you alone while we're there, but whoever is threatening you won't know that. They'll think you're alone. If they have anything in mind, they'll be dealing with me. Does that make sense?"

"Yes. So, if you're going to stay with me there, why don't you stay with me here? I have a guest room."

"I'd like that very much. Are you sure?"

"I'm sure."

He smiled. "It will be much easier to become reacquainted. Yes, I really like that idea. Just promise me one thing."

Oh, oh. What was he going to ask her to promise? "What is it?"

"I'm sticking by your side no matter where we are. The only place you'll be alone from now on is in the bathroom. Of course, your bedroom, too, but I'll be in the room closest to the door. Agreed?"

You don't know how much. "Agreed."

He took her in his arms. She stiffened a little, but not nearly as much as she had last night. "Everything will be all right. I promise. We'll take it slowly until you tell me otherwise. I hope you can learn to trust me and my judgment where this other business is concerned. I'm glad you have Craig on your side, and the reporter, too."

Her eyes met his. "But having *you* here with me means more than anything."

He moved his head slowly down and covered her lips with his. She hadn't backed away from him and he'd given her the chance to do so. He was determined to keep the kiss light, no matter how much he wanted it to blossom into more; but he swore he would not scare her away by rushing her. "I've missed you so much."

"I missed you, too." She rested her head on his shoulder. They always did fit so nicely. He was just a few inches taller than she was, but well over six feet. With her five-nine, and in heels, it was just enough to have to look up only slightly to look into his eyes. Right now, she wanted to savor the feeling of his arms around her. Could they get back what they had so long ago? He was right. They had to take this slowly, and she appreciated it, but she knew the day would come that she would lose patience with waiting and want more.

"I'll check out of the hotel and bring my things over." He lifted her chin and looked at her. "Are you sure this is what you want?" She nodded. "Come with me?"

She shook her head and tried to smile. "I have things to do." She tried to keep the mood light. "Come back whenever you want. I'll be here." She didn't want him to leave her. She wasn't exactly afraid he wouldn't come back . . . or was she? Truthfully, she wanted to be with him, but refused to give in to such a weak excuse for going along. No matter what happened from here on in, she would behave logically, rationally and most of all, maturely. She wasn't a young student anymore.

She was so glad the tour was over. In a way, this would be like starting a new life. A new and exciting life, except for the threats hanging over her head. They'd have to resolve the situation, one way or another. With Charles at her side, she had more courage than she would have alone. She didn't have to face anything alone, ever again, unless . . . No. She would *not* go there.

Laura tried to keep busy after Charles left. She told herself that she had many things that needed doing; yet she stood in the middle of the room and tried to remember what those things were. She didn't *have* to keep busy, she *wanted* to.

It was a little after three when Joyce Johnson, her neighbor, knocked on her door.

"Joyce," she said, happy to see her.

"I found this by your door the other day." She handed Laura an envelope with her name scrawled across the front.

She frowned. "How did it get here?"

"I have no idea. It must have been delivered while I was at work. Is it important?"

"I don't know." She stared at it and right away decided not to open it here.

"What's wrong? You're as white as a sheet."

She waved off Joyce's concern. "Too hectic a tour, that's all."

Joyce wasn't convinced, but she was rushed right now. She'd find out later. Still, she didn't want to be abrupt.

"How have you been? Anything new with your job?"

Joyce wore a wide smile. "I got the promotion."

"That's wonderful. Do you want to come in?"

"Some other time. I have a dinner date."

"With Phillip?"

She nodded, still smiling as she held her left hand in front of Laura's face.

"You're engaged." She hugged her friend. "I'm so happy for you."

"Thank you." She pointed at the envelope. "Maybe you have a love interest, too?"

Laura realized that she was referring to the envelope. "Well, I have, but this isn't from him. Actually, he'll be staying with me until Wednesday and then we're going back to Webster City where we went to college together."

"An old boyfriend. That's wonderful. I wish you the best of luck." She backed away. "I really have to get ready. I'll see you before you leave."

"Sure." Laura watched her go into her own door and glanced down at the envelope. Dread suddenly hit her. She wanted to see what it said, but she was going to wait until Charles was back if it killed her, and it might. She suspected that it was not a friendly note. But how would the person who wrote the others know she was here? How would they find out where she lived? It had to be something else. She put the note firmly on the coffee table and stared at it.

The intercom sounded. "Hello."

"Laura, it's Charles. Do you want to let me in?"

"Should I come down and help you carry things in?"

"No. I have what I need for now. The desk clerk said he'd have one of the men bring it over after his shift was done. It's right on his way home."

"I'll buzz you in and see you shortly." Had she really thought he might not come back? Of course not. She couldn't help smiling until she noticed the envelope on the table. They'd have to be careful not to get their fingerprints on it.

She opened the door just as Charles got there with two pieces of luggage. "Now that's service." He put them down and took off his coat. Something was wrong, She was pale and her eyes were showing . . . what? Fear? Wariness? "Is everything all right?"

She knew right away that he was perceptive enough to know something was wrong. Better get it over with. "Let me hang up your coat." As soon as she returned, she brought up the note. "I know it's silly, but just in case, we have to be careful not to smear finger prints on it in case there are any."

"You think it's another threat?"

She shrugged. "I don't know. I hope not, but what else could it be?"

He glanced at it. "Where did you find it?"

"It was by my door when my neighbor got home from work the other day."

"What day?"

"I didn't ask? What's the matter with me?" she asked berating herself for her stupidity. "Will you open it? I don't think I can. I've been staring at it since Joyce brought it over."

"Her fingerprints will be on this, you know." He carefully picked up the envelope, opened it by pulling it out from the very top and slid it onto the coffee table and they leaned over it.

It is with little patience that I say you have angered me. Rest assured that I will get you. You will not know where or when.

Laura shivered. "What does she want?"

"She?" He felt helpless as he watched her tremble. "You think Carol wrote this?"

Her laugh was bitter. "She certainly let me know that she hates me. Who else could it be?"

"I don't know, but we have to consider everything. This is a security building. How can a person get in without a key?"

"Not easily. Unless you know the person, you are told never to open the door for anyone. We can't even open it for a service repair man unless he has credentials or we know him personally." She frowned at the thought that someone here might know whoever did this. Was it Carol? Or was there someone else? Who?

"Call Craig and tell him about the note. Let him know what you think about Carol and tell him that we'll be there on Wednesday." He got up and went to the door.

"Where are you going?"

"To ask a few questions. Don't worry. I won't tell anyone what this is all about. I want to inquire who left the letter and I'll make light of it and explain it was a joke and that you want to return the favor. Maybe someone saw Carol, but I doubt she did it." He walked back to her. "Everything is too simple. If Carol is shrewd, all the circumstantial evidence would not point to her. Someone wants us to think she did it."

How could he say that? He just got back to the states and he had known nothing about any of this. Still, what if he was right? "Craig has the same feeling as I do about Carol. He just hasn't been able to find any solid evidence to support it. Without evidence, he can't charge her."

Charles put his arm around her shoulder. "If there *is* any evidence that will prove her guilt, we'll find it."

Laura leaned her head on his shoulder. "I'm so glad you're here." It wasn't that she believed him, but the feeling that she wasn't alone was welcome. She'd been alone so long, alone since the day Charles left for Paris.

He wanted to take her into his arms, but now was not the time. *Go slowly,* he told himself. He closed his eyes and enjoyed holding her. It felt wonderful. It felt right.

She lifted her head, and looked up at him. How could she be angry with him after he told her what Fredrick had said? *He said we'd go slowly.* At the time, she was thankful. It was sensible, but right now, this very minute, she wished he hadn't decided to take it slowly, not to jump back into a relationship that hadn't existed for the last six years. That didn't help her emotions, but she had to remember that Charles needed more time to regain what they had lost. Yes, she would have to move slowly for his sake. That didn't mean it would be easy.

Charles said he would be back shortly. A negative thought struck her. What if Charles wasn't sure he wanted to spend the rest of his life with her? What if he'd been in a relationship in France? He said he never married, but that didn't mean he didn't love someone else.

It wasn't long before Charles was knocking at the door. He had learned absolutely nothing. Everyone in these condos was following the rules not to let anyone in that they didn't know. A detective he wasn't, but he'd learn. He had to help Laura before those threats turned from words on a piece of paper to action. He picked up the luggage he'd left by the door. "Where should I put my luggage?" The sooner he was settled here, the sooner things might get back to normal. Well, back to *their* normal.

Laura led the way to the bedroom across the hall from hers. "It's not a large room, but it should be comfortable."

A thought struck him like a lightning bolt. He didn't want to take it slowly. He wanted to continue where they'd left off six years ago *before* Scofield had dropped his bombshell. No, even before he'd made up his mind to go to Paris, he could have handled the whole thing differently. He could have been more sympathetic to Laura's dream. He could have realized what it meant to her. If he hadn't been such a self-centered hot shot back then, he would have cared about *her* dream as much as he cared about his own. He had to chalk that up to youth, but down deep, he knew that he was unable to accept just how selfish his actions had been. No, he had to take it slowly for her sake. He had to convince her that he'd changed; that he'd grown up and could see things clearly now.

The room was more than ample. The different shades of green were restful and large yellow flowers were nestled between the green leaves of the bedspread and draperies. "This is very pretty, Laura."

"Not exactly masculine, but not totally feminine, either."

"It's very nice. You always did have a good sense of colors."

She remembered watching him paint and she'd paid special attention to the different hues of each color. She noticed how he painted the different greens that he used when painting mountains and trees. "I had a good teacher."

"Next thing you'll tell me is that you started to paint. Did you?"

She laughed. "Hardly. I couldn't draw a simple square house or make a tree that didn't look like a misshapen bush. No, I stuck to my music."

"I'm glad. If it's possible, you play with more feeling now than you did in college, not to mention your compositions."

She lowered her head. "I needed an outlet for my turbulent emotions." She shrugged. "You might have been able to tell which pieces were sad and angry and which ones were memories of better times."

He reached for her. "I'm so sorry that I believed Scofield. I should have known better. Can you ever forgive me?"

She looked into his eyes. "We were young then. Who knows if we'd have made the same mistakes now that we did then?" She took a deep breath. "Maybe we should do as you suggested and start again."

"It's more easily said than done when you love someone so completely. Can you forget the past?"

She thought for a moment. "I can try. I can't help but think that we've changed in ways we'd never think about. We can make getting to know each other a pleasant pastime, not a necessary undertaking."

He nodded. "You're right. From this day forward, we'll speak not of six years ago, but of the people we've become. Sound good?"

"It sounds very sensible."

"And I'd like to think that we are more sensible."

Chapter 6

Laura walked through the gallery and studied each and every painting. They were incredible. In college, his pictures portrayed what he wanted them to, but now they went far beyond that. Except for the Eifel Tower, when her taxi sped by it on tour, she had never seen the places he painted. She had seen pictures of the Eifel Tower, and had seen it often in movies, but she was in awe as she stood in front of the painting. She couldn't take her eye off it. The background was utter perfection. Why had she never noticed the beauty of the Eifel Tower? She knew why. Her heart had been broken and she wanted nothing to do with the city where Charles had chosen to study. The sooner she got away from France, the better off she felt she would be.

She walked around, studying each painting. She recognized the Cathedral of Notre-Dame and several scenes from places unknown to her. Particularly impressive were scenes from the spectacular Champs-Elysees and the Arc De Triomphe. She returned to the Eifel Tower painting. As exquisite as they were, none could compare with this one.

"Oh, my," said an older woman standing beside her, "isn't that the most beautiful sight you've ever seen?" She was dressed in a deep purple dress, furs and jewels which dominated her appearance. She pointed to the very top of the picture. "It brings back such memories. I met my late husband right there."

"Then you've been to Paris," Laura said enviously.

"Oh my, yes. You haven't?"

Sadness overtook Laura. "I've been to Paris, but it didn't mean much to me then."

The woman looked at her with disbelief. How could anyone see the Eifel Tower and not be thrilled? "I must say, I can not imagine visiting Paris and not be taken in by all the beauty it has to offer."

Laura nodded. "It wasn't a good time for me." She hadn't intended to part with that information, but she felt the need to defend herself. Before she had a chance to say anything else, Charles was beside her.

"I take it I have your approval?" He pointed to the painting.

The woman spoke excitedly. "My dear man, you are the artist?"

"Guilty as charged."

"It's absolutely brilliant. I was just telling the young lady that it took me back thirty years. I met my late husband there." Again she pointed to the top of the tower.

"I simply must have it."

Charles smiled. "I hope it will bring back many pleasant memories for you."

"Oh, it will. It really will." She rushed off to find the owner of the gallery,

Charles chuckled. "It never ceases to please me when I get a reaction like that."

"And why shouldn't you? These are breathtaking, Charles. I knew you were good, but these are . . . beyond excellence." She shook her head. "No, there really is no word that can describe them. I'm so very proud of you."

"No more proud than I was when I heard you play, especially when you played your own compositions. They left me speechless."

She spotted a scene in which a man was in a row boat. His back was to the viewer. "This scene looks sad, Charles. The man seems lonely."

He nodded. That's me, all alone without my love."

She lowered her head so he couldn't see her eyes. He painted what he felt, too. He'd always been emotional. This was not the time to confess that she, too, had written what she felt. That she had used her music to express her sorrow, her anger and even her resignation. He'd left her and her devastation brought out the music that others heard as simply emotional. Few were able to pinpoint exactly what she'd felt at any given time. That is not to say that they didn't feel the emotion, but some of it was hidden in the harmony, or in the beautiful strains of a melody. She had interspersed the less depressed ones with some of her memories of Charles. Those memories had resulted in pure beauty. Most people, musicians or not, seemed to understand those few pieces.

"When did you write them?" he asked, curious about her past.

She shrugged. "I don't know," she wanted to mislead him. That surprised her. Why didn't she want him to know how devastated she'd been? "During the past five or six years. Why?"

"Because your music would probably follow the same pattern as my paintings."

He knew? Of course he did. How could he not know if he'd experienced the same despair? She straightened up and walked to the next painting. This was no the time to discuss the past. Maybe there would never be a time for it.

They spent two more hours at the gallery, listening to all the comments that were proof of the overwhelming success of the showing.

As they walked to the car, he looked closely at the slip of paper the owner had given him of the paintings sold. "I think I may be even wealthier than I had hoped. Paul priced some of the painting much higher than I would have.

"Surely he knows what people will pay. I mean, he owns the gallery. He certainly must charge what he thinks they are worth."

"I suppose. I sold several in France through the years, but never at prices like these. I can't say that I ever translated the French currency to the US dollar. No," he shook his head, "I never thought of that money in terms of our dollar."

She smiled. "Maybe you were too busy painting to care what they sold for."

He nodded. "For awhile, I was just happy that someone bought them." He thought back to the many tourists that stopped by and asked how much they were. He would shrug and give them some figure that assured his next meal, and not much more. Some of the tourists looked like they didn't have enough money to indulge in art. He was doing them a favor, in a way.

"Oh, Charles," she put her hand on his arm, "you thought so little of your talent?"

"No, not really. I thought about when we went window shopping and knew very well that we couldn't afford the things we dreamed of having."

She leaned closer and gave him a slight hug. "Always considerate. That's one of the things I loved about you."

He smiled. "Tell me more, but not right now." He pointed to the car and helped her in. He closed her door and went around to the other side and slid behind the wheel. "As you were saying?"

She laughed. "You heard very well what I was saying." She took a deep breath. "Craig was quite upset about the note."

"Why didn't you tell me that before?"

"Because you had a showing today. Why should I take the chance of upsetting you? Today was your special day and nothing should interfere with it."

"Now, who's being considerate?" He reached over and covered her hand with his. "Tell me what he said."

"He was concerned about my safety. I told him that you were staying with me."

"And what did he say about that?"

She smiled to herself. "He was glad that I wasn't alone, and even happier to learn it was you staying with me." In fact, she could hear in his voice how happy he was, not just for her safety, but because they were together again. She called him an old romantic. He agreed and told her that he and Lydia were celebrating their fortieth anniversary next month. Would she and Charles ever get to forty years? Would they be together after this whole thing was over? She wanted to believe it, but she had reservations. If only he would talk about the last six years. Oh, he'd talked about them, all right, but had never once mentioned a woman.

"What are you thinking?" he asked.

"Just mulling over a bunch of things in my mind."

"Are you worried about the note?"

"It's a bit of a shock every time I get one, but I can't say I'm shaking in my boots. Of course, that could be because you're with me."

"I only hope I can live up to your expectations."

She chuckled. "What expectations? As far as I'm concerned, Carol will think twice about doing anything when I'm not alone. Besides, do you expect her to break into my condo and stab me in my sleep or something?"

His expression turned solemn. "Don't joke about it, Laura."

"I'm sorry, but the fact that you're with me makes me feel confident that nothing is going to happen."

"Well, let's hope that you're right."

A short time later, he pulled into the underground garage and parked in her assigned space. As he turned toward her, he wanted the closeness they'd had years ago, but he knew it was too soon. Better to get this business with Scofield's death and the threats settled. After that, he would wait for nothing. She would have to listen to him and giver him an answer, preferably the one he wanted so desperately to hear. He was suddenly aware that she was watching him as he stared at her.

"What are you thinking?" she asked.

"I'm thinking that it is so nice to sit here and get my fill of your beauty."

Oh, how she wanted to believe that, but his expression had been so urgent, so serious, she didn't know if she could. "That's all?"

He laughed. "Isn't that enough? I had six long years without you, Laura. Is it so hard to believe that I want to feast my eyes on you?"

She felt the heat creep up from her neck to her face. She'd have thought she was beyond the age of blushing, but he managed to prove her wrong. She thought about what he'd said. "No, it isn't hard to believe because I feel the same way about you. I want to spend my time just watching you."

"There," he said as he kissed her forehead, "you see; the feeling is mutual." He opened the door, but didn't get out right away. "We'll leave for Webster City in the morning. Will your reputation be in jeopardy if I'm with you?"

"In this day and age? Hardly. We'll have the suite and a room. Who will know?"

"Hopefully I won't be seen entering your suite. We need to keep it secret."

"What's the plan?" Amusement lit up her eyes. He got out of the car to come around to her side. He helped her out. "We'll speak when we get into your condo. You never know who's lurking around the corner, listening to our every word."

She shivered. "I wish you wouldn't say things like that." Just then, they heard footsteps in the corner of the garage, but they couldn't see anyone.

They stood perfectly still. "You can't be too careful," he whispered. "Let's go." He put his hand on her back and guided her to the door which took them to her condo.

As soon as they were inside her unit, he locked both locks. She'd noticed that he'd made it a point to look around while they were still in the garage. That didn't exactly put her at ease. She'd always felt quite safe here. Was she wrong?

Charles relaxed after he'd checked every room. The door was sturdy and since they were not on the first floor, he was quite certain they'd remain alone without uninvited guests. "If someone is watching you, they know you're not alone." He took off his coat and hung it into the hall closet.

"Do you think whoever was in the garage was watching me?"

No point in making her jumpy. If someone was watching them, he didn't want them to know that he was on to them. "It was probably someone who lives here. You'll have to forgive my imagination, Laura."

She hung her coat beside his. "And I always thought you were a realist. You painted only what you saw. That doesn't leave room for imagination."

"True, but you have to leave me an outlet someplace. It might as well be my fantasy of being a world famous sleuth." He grinned, hoping he had discouraged some of her fear.

"And I suppose my name is Watson?"

He laughed. "You're the prettiest Watson I ever saw."

"In that case, come and help me solve a mystery."

He frowned. "Which mystery is that?"

"We have to find something to eat. I didn't provide much because we'll be leaving in the morning."

"Don't tell me you still eat something before you go to bed."

She nodded. "Every night."

He studied her figure. "Without gaining a single pound. Lucky you."

She stuck her chin in the air. "Luck is not involved. It is sheer . . . well, if you must know, I lead a pretty active life while I'm on tour. There are times when I hardly get to sit down to a dinner."

"That doesn't sound like the most pleasant way to spend your time. Do you really like touring the world?"

"Yes and no. I love it for the first two months; after that, it gets tiresome and taxing. By the end of the tour, I don't want to see a train or an airplane. I like to drive whenever I can, so I can have some quiet time. I need that."

He nodded as he put his hands on her shoulders and drew her toward him. "You would love my life for about a week. I live in seclusion and rarely see others unless I'm painting a particular scene." He kissed her nose. "Maybe we could share. We could spend two months of your life to every two weeks of mine. What do you think?"

Was he serious? It sounded like he had plans for their future. If only he knew she'd give up the tours in the blink of her eye to spend the rest of her life with him. She would always find an outlet for her music and he would never deny her that just as she would never deny him his painting. "I'd call that a compromise."

She went into the kitchen to avoid any further talk on the subject. First things first, and that meant dealing with Carol and what was happening in Webster City.

They stopped at a lovely chalet-like lodge just outside of Webster City. It was new in recent years, so neither one had been there before. Laura loved experiencing something new with Charles. If it was a good experience, they were ecstatic. If it was terrible, they laughed it off vowing never to go back. If it was just passable, they hoped that the establishment would learn from the information they'd filled in on the cards that the waitress gave them to fill out.

The restaurant was located by a lake with a grove of trees on the side and a hill in the back. There were windows all around so one could revel in the view no matter where they sat. They boasted excellent food and impeccable service. All in all, Laura thought it was wonderful to experience it with Charles just after they found each other again.

Charles noticed the painting in the waiting area. He would have to look closer, but he was almost certain that he saw the scene of Lake Corry he had painted as a student.

He studied Laura. She looked as beautiful as ever, but her movements were quick, as if she were nervous. "Relax, Laura. Enjoy the ambience."

She smiled. "I do enjoy it, but I can't help wondering what I'm getting you into." She shook her head. "I should never have told you about the threats."

"I would have found out. Let's enjoy ourselves while we can. There's no one here that even knows you. Look around. Do you see anyone you know?"

She looked around. "No, but--"

He covered her hand with his. "Six years is a long time to remember a familiar face. Do you realize how many students come here to study and go their separate ways every year? I doubt that the locals form lasting relationships with them."

"I'm sure you're right."

"How many people at the concert remembered you from before?"

"I requested no party after the concert, so only a few spoke with me. I did, however, see a few instructors who were here when we attended college."

"Six years isn't long for teachers. I suppose they settle in after a few years and have no wish to move on."

She sighed. "It's a big undertaking to remember that many names. One teacher probably has to remember hundreds of students each year. That's a lot of names to remember."

The waiter brought their salads and refilled their water glasses. They ate in silence, admiring the variety of unusual ingredients in the salad. It was a comfortable silence, a silence in which they enjoyed each other.

When their meals came, they were beautifully presented. Her walleye was excellently prepared and was resting on a bed of greens with couscous on the side. Charles had ordered beef stroganoff served on egg noodles.

When they were almost finished, a man had approached their table and stood beside Laura. "We meet again."

"Professor Standish," she exclaimed.

"How nice to see you again, Miss Westlund." He turned to Charles. "And Mr. Templeton, isn't it?"

"Yes." Charles extended his hand which the professor shook.

"Miss Westlund and I ran into each other last week."

"Yes, I remember. You wanted to see Chief Thomas about your nephew," she said. "I trust everything turned out all right."

"Not exactly." He turned to Charles. "Eduardo is extremely acerbic. He's vitriolic and . . . well, nothing like the rest of my family. We come from a most fortuitous primogeniture; yet, he's malevolent, licentious, and fractious." He threw up his hands as if to rid himself of his problem. "Recently, he's become somewhat of a sycophant. One never knows what to expect next." He shook his head trying to shake his mood. "Forgive me. I tend to ramble on about things I don't understand."

Laura glanced at Charles who was trying his best not to laugh. She looked away as she spoke. "I'm sorry to hear of your problems."

"They *are* mine, are they not? I should never have promised my sister . . . Well, enough of that! It was very nice seeing both of you again." He bowed his head slightly, turned and left.

Laura watched until he had left the building. "All right, go ahead and laugh."

Charles chuckled. "He's unbelievable."

"You never had a class from him, did you?"

"Fortunately, no. How did you stand to listen to him for an hour?"

"It was awful at first, but after a while, we finally got the idea that he wanted us to bring dictionaries and look up the meanings. Most of us wrote down the words as he used them and looked them up after class."

"What was his point?"

She smiled. "It was a good one and it proved to be legitimate. The class was designed primarily for those going into theater. Actors have to know what words mean before they can read lines well enough to be believable. They often go to an audition, are handed a script and read the lines. They don't have a chance to look it over first."

Charles nodded. "All right. You convinced me. The professor had good reason to use his vocabulary in class, but does he have to carry it over into his every day life?" Nobody would want to live with a man like that. "Is he married?"

"He was six years ago. I don't know about now."

Charles laughed. "If he always speaks like that, I'd guess he no longer is."

Laura smiled. "I see what you mean, but he's not a bad person."

"I know. He's a bit self-centered, but many men in his position are." Charles took a last sip of his water. "Are we ready to leave?"

"Yes. It was a wonderful meal, Charles. I really enjoyed it, but that has to do with the company as well as the ambience."

"Let's not forget the food."

"That goes without saying." She folded her napkin and placed it on the table. "I don't think this place was here six years ago."

"I'm sure it wasn't. I often drove this route out of Webster City when I went to visit my grandparents." Charles took out his credit card and the waiter came to the table immediately. He took the card and left. When he returned, he placed the check and the card in front of Charles to sign.

"Thank you, sir," said the waiter with obvious delight.

"You're welcome." He had left a large tip since they tied up their table for so long. He felt it only right when the waiter might have served at least two more couples during the time they sat talking.

They walked out to the car. "It will be nice to see the college again."

"They're thinking of changing the name of the college," said Laura.

"Why is that?"

"You know, of course, the story about how the school was started."

Charles nodded. "If I remember correctly, it started as a school for fine arts and music for high school juniors and seniors."

"Yes. It was small and never had many students. Somewhere in the 50's, Rita Hallmark, a famous actress moved to Webster City and bought a large building and started a theater. She starred in most of the plays, and she was able to stir up interest in the residents. Soon, the adults who acted in the productions wanted their children to have instruction in theater. Miss Hallmark funded the change from a school to a college and was responsible for bringing in only the best actors to do the teaching. When they added musicals to the productions, it became the Webster College of Arts and Music. A few years later, they started to take music instruction seriously."

Charles nodded. "Soon, it became the Hallmark College of Arts and Music, extending *Arts* to include sculpting and painting."

"You've got it." She smiled. "That was a rather long explanation. I'm sorry."

He stopped, put his hands on her shoulders and turned her to face him. "Never apologize for that. You were always very thorough and detailed. That's one of the things I loved about you."

She looked down, so touched by his remark that she wanted so badly for him to put his arms around her and hold her like he had so many years ago. This was not working. He wanted to take things slowly and she was ready to throw herself into his arms. She'd have to practice self discipline more than she was now. "You used to call me long winded."

"A term of endearment." He kissed her cheek and dropped his hands. He'd been ready to kiss her, and not like a brother. Best not to remember their past or the word *slow* was bound to have very little meaning.

She laughed, embarrassed because of her strong feelings which he might not have. He wanted slow and as much as she didn't want it that way, that's what he'd get. She only hoped that they'd have enough to do to keep them distracted until he decided enough was enough and give in to the feelings they had once had for each other.

It was just past two when they drove into Webster City. They went right to the hotel and checked in. As they went to the elevator, a woman approached.

"Laura Westlund?" She was heavy set and shorter than Laura. Her hair was jet black right out of a bottle. "My goodness, but it's been a long time. How are you?"

"Miss Compton." She shook hands with her. "Do you remember Charles Templeton?"

She studied him. "I'm not sure, although the name is familiar. Were you in my sight reading class?"

He smiled. "No, Miss Compton. Music was never my field."

Laura spoke up proudly. "Charles is a painter."

"I see." She looked away. "Well, you certainly can't paint in this weather." She pointed outside. It had started to rain in sheets.

"No, Miss Compton. He's an artist. He paints pictures, not houses."

She laughed. "Well, of course. I was just joking with you."

They all laughed, but Laura thought of all the times Miss Compton had made a mistake and explained it away as a joke. She not only seemed older, but confused. No, it was more than that. Her eyes looked . . . blank. Strange.

"With whom are you studying, Laura?"

She was taken aback. Something was definitely wrong here. Before she could think of something to say, a young woman ran up to them.

"Aunt Maude, There you are." She took her by the hand and tried to lead her away from Laura and Charles. "I'm so sorry. I turned my head for only a moment, and she was gone. Come along now, Aunt Maude. We have to be at the clinic in ten minutes. We'll just make it."

"Yes, dear." She glanced at Laura. "My jailor." She nodded to her niece. She smiled and went arm in arm with her.

Laura frowned. "What do you suppose is wrong?"

"If I had one guess, I'd say Alzheimer's is setting in." He shook his head sadly as they watched her leave the building.

"You're probably right." She sighed. "You know, she used to claim that she was joking to cover a mistake in judgment." She smiled. "Do you remember Joe Colton?"

Charles thought. "I don't think so."

"Well, he majored in piano, organ and voice, so he had her for three classes. He became her pet. He was skinny and shorter than most guys in the class. She was always heavy, and she asked Joe to use his lunch hour to do her paper work. When he said he needed to eat lunch, she said she didn't get to eat lunch, so why should he? He always answered that he was skinny and that she wasn't." She chuckled. "You know, she was never liked by her students, but to see her like this ... "

"Poetic justice?"

"Even that thought is cruel."

He pressed the button calling the elevator. When the elevator door opened, they went inside. "You don't think she's still teaching, do you?"

"How could she?" At least, she hoped not.

"Was Webster City her home?"

"I don't know. Probably. Anyone who taught here for fifteen years probably made this their home, don't you think?"

"Makes sense unless she had family elsewhere."

"She was never married. Her parents would be long gone, so all that remains would be siblings." She shrugged. "It's sad to see her this way."

"It's sad to see anyone that way."

They arrived at the suite first. Charles went on to his room while Laura entered the suite. It was the same suite she'd had before. After putting her suitcase down and taking off her coat, she glanced at the sofa bed, hoping that it would be more comfortable than most hide-a-beds. She didn't like the thought of Charles sleeping uncomfortably while trying to protect her. In a way, she didn't want to think of him sleeping in the next room. If she dreamed about him before, how much more intense would those dreams be now? The thought was not pleasant. She loved him dearly so it was no puzzle to understand her reluctance to yearn for what she might never have again.

Charles came in and looked around. "This is a comfortable suite. I think it will serve our purpose."

"I only hope you don't expect too much from that sofa bed." She pointed at the sofa. Although it was plush and well padded, that didn't mean the mattress would be comfortable.

"Don't worry," he said patting her arm. "I'm sure it will do very well."

Laura took a minute to call Craig and then Brad. Craig said he'd see her in a day or two. Brad asked if they could meet this afternoon. She covered the receiver and looked up at Charles. "Do you mind if we meet with Brad later this afternoon?"

"I think it's a good idea."

"Four o'clock would be fine, Brad. Do you want to come here?"

"I'd rather we met at Carlson's coffee shop on the edge of town. I'm seeing too many people who know me and the hotel is in the center of town. Do you mind?"

"No. That's probably smart. You know, I don't think I'm ready for this cloak and dagger stuff."

He laughed. "It isn't that bad, but I don't want people to see us together and surmise that we're chummy with each other."

"Don't worry." She laughed. "We'll just be friends. People won't know if you know Charles or me."

"Four o'clock it is." In a gangster voice, he said, "I'll wear a tan trench coat."

She laughed before she hung up.

Charles looked at her out of the corner of his eyes. "Cloak and dagger stuff?"

She shrugged. "You know, the stuff they do in the movies."

"God forbid. I hope you aren't serious."

She laughed, but wasn't all together sure she wasn't serious. She shivered every time she thought of the threats. She'd been able to forget about them for a while, thanks to Charles; but now they were here, and that meant they were in the middle of the mess.

"Will I be seeing Carol at all?"

"I don't know. Brad is more or less running the show."

He laughed. "You're scaring me now. You even talk like a gumshoe."

"A what?"

"Never mind. I'm going to hang up my clothes and freshen up." He looked at his watch. "I'll pick you up in fifteen minutes, if that's enough time."

"Plenty, but we'll be too early to meet Brad. "

"I thought we'd run by a grocery store and stock the little refrigerator." He pointed to where it sat. "You'll need something at bedtime," he teased.

"Coffee is furnished, but an evening snack is always in order for those of us who developed the bad habit."

His teeth were clamping down on his lower lip. He might as well confess. "I-ah-adopted the habit in Paris." Actually, he'd spent evening after evening thinking about Laura. It was foolish, but he did it as a remembrance, a foolish act honoring her habit.

She'd watched his eyes when he spoke. There was a tenderness that she hadn't seen since he left for Paris. It made her feel week in the knees. Did he still have that kind of power over her? And if so, she could only hope that he felt half of what she felt for him. *Go slowly.* She had trouble remembering that. If only . . .

After picking up a few groceries, they entered the coffee shop at three-fifty-five. Brad was already sitting in the back booth where they couldn't be overheard. There were only a few people there at this time, and it looked like they had finished their food. Brad was smart in choosing this place and the time.

Laura made the introductions and they ordered coffee.

"What have you learned?"

Brad grinned. "Not as much as I wanted to, but I have a few facts." He took out a small notebook and glanced at the page. "Al Freeman has been too tied up to speak with me. I thought we could try together tomorrow."

"I thought you were going to see him last week."

"*He* decided against it."

Laura frowned. "He doesn't know why you really want to see him, does he?"

Brad was thoughtful. "I wonder. Don't forget, he's involved with Carol, and by now, Carol might wonder if that little SUV incident is behind this."

Charles asked, "Why would she suspect that?"

"Just a hunch. If she sent the threats and if she was driving the SUV, she might put two and two together."

"Laura got another threat in Chicago." Charles wasn't sure Brad knew that.

"Craig told me. How the devil would anyone know where to find you?"

"Brad, I'm in the Chicago phone book."

"But how would they know when you'd be there? Did you tell anyone here?"

"I'm sure I mentioned it to Craig, but I don't remember if I even mentioned the concert in Chicago to anyone else."

Charles answered. "It wasn't hard for me to find out that she had a concert in Chicago and I'd just arrived there from Paris. I'm sure anyone could find out with a phone call or by looking at the entertainment section of the paper."

"You flew in from Paris?"

"Charles studied with a master painter there. He's an artist," she added proudly.

"Ah." Brad nodded having figured out that Charles was the one Carol referred to when she told him all about their love for each other and his sudden departure for Paris. When she'd spoken, it was with bitterness. Did Carol fancy herself in love with Charles, too? It was entirely possible that Carol was trying to point a finger at Charles by saying she wondered if he actually left for Paris when he had. She implied that he might have stayed to save his true love from a life with an old man. He turned to Charles. "You're the artist who left her high and dry."

Charles could feel his face redden, although he wasn't sure how much was from embarrassment and how much was anger. What else could he expect?

"Brad," Laura put her hand on Brad's arm, hoping to save bad feelings. "Shortly before Charles left, Fredrick told him that he'd asked me to marry him and that I accepted his proposal."

Brad sat up straighter. "You didn't tell me that."

"I didn't find out until Charles came to see me after the concert in Chicago. It wasn't until a stagehand called me *Miss Westlund* that he asked me why I didn't use my married name. That's when he told me about Fredrick's lies."

Brad frowned. "What did Scofield have to gain?"

Charles knew. "He wanted me out of the way, and he got his way."

"You didn't check his story?"

Charles again blushed. "What can I say? I was young."

Brad accepted that, thinking of the foolishness of his own youth. "There were a couple other people who despised Scofield, but people don't remember names. Six years is a long time to remember names, dates and times."

Laura nodded. "I can understand that. I sometimes have trouble remembering what I did last week."

I've asked those I interviewed to try to associate other things with Scofield. If they think of anything, they'll call me."

"I'm not sure I know how you mean."

Brad looked at her. "Say I asked you if anyone gave you flowers while you were here. You'd say yes. I'd say what time was that? You would associate the time with the end of your performance. Another question is when did you get the threatening notes?"

She took a deep breath. "I see what you mean. I may not have any idea, except I can associate it with the concert, the hotel suite, and make a better decision as to time."

"Right. There are better examples, but you get the picture."

"Funny thing," Brad offered, "some of Scofield's former students think Carol resented you, but resented Scofield even more. They commented that she had a very volatile personality back then. Do you remember seeing anything like that about her?"

She took a deep breath, giving her time to think back. "Not then. All I can remember is that she resented me because I got the award and later, the contract for the concert tour. She hated me, but I don't remember her reaction to Fredrick."

"Think about it," said Charles. "If she hated you, and she had a thing for Scofield that wasn't returned, wouldn't she resent him as well?"

"It's possible, I suppose, but wouldn't she hate me because she'd think it was my fault for taking his attention from her? When you're young, I suppose it's hard to understand why someone doesn't return your feelings."

"That was my thought. Besides, I remember Carol." Charles cringed. "She was no one's sweetheart."

Brad sighed. "Still isn't, unless you can count Al Freeman. I haven't been able to interview him, yet. I can't help thinking that Al is avoiding me."

"When will Craig get involved?"

Brad shrugged. "If and when I have anything concrete. My questions concern honoring Scofield. Craig's would be police business. He doesn't want to tip his hand.

They talked for a while before Brad stood up. "I have an appointment to see a Jerry Paulson at five-thirty. I'd better be on my way. I'll keep you posted and you let me know what you learn. Call me anytime." He held out his hand to Charles. "Nice meeting you." They shook hands and Brad left.

Chapter 7

Charles and Laura were on their way out of the coffee shop when a man bumped into Charles.

"Watch where you're going, hotshot."

Charles was surprised because he'd been minding his own business and it seemed to him that this man had deliberately bumped into him. Charles immediately checked to see that his wallet was still where it belonged. In France, pickpockets often bumped into you to cover a theft. The victim wouldn't even feel the removal of his wallet because he was distracted by the thief bumping into him. "I believe it was you who was not watching where you were walking."

"Stuff it, man." He took a second look at Laura and frowned. "Well if it isn't teacher's pet." His words couldn't have sounded nastier if he'd been a ten year old delinquent.

Laura studied him, knowing that she'd known him before. Finally, she remembered. "Ed Langston?"

"Yeah, right. Never thought a prima donna would remember little old me."

"No need to get belligerent," said Charles.

"Nobody tells me what to do, bud. Butt out." He turned back to Laura. "So Scofield's pet came back to the scene of the crime."

"What crime is that?" Charles wanted to get this man talking. If he knew about the supposed crime that was labeled a suicide, it might behoove them to listen to him.

"Were you born without a brain? Scofield's murder. What else?"

"I thought it was suicide."

He nodded angrily. "Sure. She," he designated Laura, "wanted us to think that."

Charles clenched his hands into fists. "Now wait just a minute--"

"No." His hand flew up as he pointed a finger at Charles. "You wait."

Chief Thomas entered the coffee shop and headed right for them when he'd heard a loud voice. "Oh no," he mumbled under his breath. "Not this guy again."

Ed saw him and started to walk away. "I'm leaving, Mr. Chief of Police." He laughed as he walked out the door.

"What was that all about?" he asked Laura.

"I'm not sure. Craig, this is Charles Templeton."

Craig smiled as he offered his hand. "Nice meeting you." They shook hands and he turned to Laura. "Got a minute?"

"Sure. Do you want to go back in and sit down?"

He shook his head. "No, it won't take long. I just want to catch you up on a couple of things."

"Something new?" she asked.

"I found out that Carol wasn't out of town after Brad interviewed her. She couldn't have delivered the note in Chicago. She has an alibi for that entire day."

"A reliable alibi?"

"I'd say so. She was judging at an all day music festival at the high school."

Laura nodded. "That's legitimate enough. Does that mean that she's no longer a suspect?"

"I wouldn't say that. She does have a dark green SUV and it was possible that she left three of the notes. She could have had someone else deliver the last note. That's as much as I've learned except . . ."

"Except what?"

"Scofield's death. Brad has reported that a few former students considered Carol a threat to her piano teacher. It might be that she wasn't in love with him after all. Or," he spoke while he was thinking, "she didn't like the fact that he fancied himself husband material for you and didn't return *her* feelings. It's only a matter of time before I reopen that suicide."

"Do you really think Carol is capable of murder?"

"I don't know. She had a violent temper. Remember she was young then."

"Weren't we all?" muttered Charles.

"Well, that's about it. I don't want to tip my hand until after I have a few more facts. Six years is a long time for people to remember."

"Brad mentioned the same thing. I can appreciate that."

Craig put on his hat. "Anyway, I'm glad I caught you." He turned to Charles. "Nice seeing you again, Templeton."

Again? Charles nodded but didn't say anything. He didn't remember actually talking to the Chief of Police six years ago, but of course, he knew who he was.

"Nice fellow," Charles commented after the chief had left.

"I don't know what I would have done without him. He took me under his wing." She chuckled. "I never was sure if it was his idea or if his wife made him do it."

"If he hadn't wanted to do it, I doubt his wife could have made him. He strikes me as being his own man."

"Instead of hen-pecked, you mean?" Her expression turned angry. "Do I understand that remark to mean women should take the back seat in a marriage?"

Charles laughed. "I said nothing of the kind, but you must know that some men will not be told what to do."

"I doubt that his wife *told* him. I think she would suggest it and he would then do as he felt best."

Charles was still grinning. "I'm sure you're right."

"Charles, you're laughing at me."

He sobered. "No. I'm teasing you. I used to love teasing you. Remember?"

Her anger dissipated. "How could I forget? If it wasn't one thing, it was another." Her face softened with the memory of his joking with her. He'd always made her laugh when she'd been in a bad mood. "We're grown up now."

"So we are. I guess we have to give in to our grouchy moods."

She good naturedly hit him on his shoulder. They reached the car and he held the door for her before going around to the driver's side. He started the engine, but turned to face her. "This character that bumped into me. He definitely does not like you, Laura."

"I'm well aware of that."

"Who is he?"

"Well," Laura thought back, "he was Fredrick's star pupil for all of two months."

"Only two months? What happened?"

She shrugged. "Ed happened. You saw how belligerent he was to me. One day, he suddenly turned from Dr, Jekyll to Mr. Hyde, or vice versa. Whatever. It's strange. He seemed nice enough when he first started college. He was two years behind me, so I didn't see him all that often, but I did hear him play once in a while and he was very good. I would imagine something traumatic happened to him to cause such a change in him. Fredrick was thrilled with his talent at first. Then, Ed turned sour. He said Ed could have been the best student he'd ever had if he would have taken his studies seriously. By the end of the semester, Fredrick refused to teach him. He insisted that Miss Compton take over Ed's piano lessons. Ed never forgave Fredrick." Laura frowned.

"What is it?"

"I'm remembering something. A few days before my graduation, Ed came out of Fredrick's office, really angry. He was yelling foul language and Fredrick finally slammed the door in his face. Ed said 'I'll get you for this, Scofield,' and he fled down the hall. I've never seen anyone quite that angry."

"What caused the anger?"

She shook her head. "I don't think Fredrick ever told me. In fact, he never mentioned Ed's name again that I remember."

Charles was silent for a moment. "Do you realize that Ed could have killed Scofield? At the very least he'll be a suspect if he doesn't have an alibi."

She sighed. "I never thought about it." She sat up a little straighter. "I'd better call Craig when we get to the hotel and tell him what happened."

He nodded and they drove off.

They ate in the hotel dining room. Charles suggested they sit close to the door in front of the room where everyone could see them. If anyone wanted to harm her, they'd probably try when they knew she was alone. Sooner or later, someone would be careless and make a mistake so they'd find out who was doing this. He wanted this whole thing to be over so he and Laura could get on with their lives . . . together.

Having finished a nice meal, they returned to their rooms. Charles told her he would slip into her room when he wouldn't be seen.

Laura dialed Craig's number and informed him about Ed Langston.

"He's always been a trouble maker. You know that as well as I do, Laura."

"I guess I never thought about it. Actually, I never thought about him much at all until Fredrick mentioned that Ed was a promising student, possibly the best student he'd ever taught."

"You'd think the boy would appreciate that kind of praise."

"Yes, but two months later, Fredrick became disenchanted with him."

"So he might have done something to anger Scofield?"

She thought about it. "I had the impression that Fredrick had done something to anger Ed. I don't know. Maybe it was a mutual dislike by that time."

"Dislike? You said his face was . . . how did you put it? Oh, yes, hatred personified."

"True. What do you think?"

"I think Ed Langston is going to get a visit from me. I'll question him without telling him what we suspect. Laura, you know I can't charge him with anything unless I have hard evidence. If I find that he doesn't have an alibi for the night Scofield was killed, I'll question him about the times you received the threats. I won't reveal the reason because I can't just associate him with the threats on a general suspicion."

"Do you think he was responsible for them?"

Craig was silent for a moment. "One thing at a time. Let's take this slowly."

Where did I hear that before? Just then, Charles used his key to slip into the suite. When he saw she was on the phone, he put his briefcase down and took out a pair of cobalt blue pajamas and grinned at her.

She bit her lip to keep from laughing. "You will keep us informed, won't you, Craig?"

"Of course. Be careful. If Scofield's death was murder, you could be in more danger than I thought. I'm glad Templeton is with you."

"Yes. So am I."

"I'll keep in touch. Don't come to the police station to see me. We don't want anyone to get the idea that we suspect anything. I'll call you. We can meet someplace by accident."

"All right. Thank you, Craig."

"No problem. Watch your back, Laura. Goodbye." He hung up.

Charles sat in the chair next to hers. "What does he think?"

"He's going to question Ed. He'll keep in touch, but he doesn't want us to go to the police station. He thinks it would tip our hand."

"He's right. So, you and I will be like twins joined at the hip until this is over. Can you handle it?"

She smiled. "Oh, I think I can manage . . . somehow." She put the phone book back into the drawer next to the Bible. "Do you really wear those pajamas to bed?"

He laughed, "Where else would I wear them?"

"That isn't what I meant."

He feigned hurt feelings. "You don't like my pajamas?"

"It . . . it just doesn't seem like something you'd wear."

He raised an eyebrow. "Just what kind of pajamas do you think suit my personality?"

"Hmmm," she made it a point to think about it. "Probably a pair with a scene of a beautiful sunset or the Eiffel Tower."

He nodded. "Why wouldn't I paint my own scene?" He shook his head as he chuckled. "Next time, I'll take you shopping with me."

"You bought those just for wearing here?"

His eyes closed to slits and he was talking from one side of his mouth. He was in gangster mode. "You wanna make somthin' of it?"

She laughed. "I didn't realize how much I missed your impersonations. This takes me back six years."

"We were never in a hotel room together six years ago." His words were short and clipped.

Her instinct was to back off, but she stopped herself. She'd always been proper, if not the picture of innocence. She hoped she had matured since then. "I was talking about your impersonations." She laughed softly. "The one I liked best was Donald Duck."

The lines in his face smoothed out and the harshness was gone. "You flatter me," he said in his duck voice. He turned serious. "Let's not forget that the reason we're here is no joking matter. We have to be on our toes every minute."

"I know. Craig said much the same thing."

"What do you want to do until it's time for bed?"

"I don't know," she said as she tried to avoid looking into the bedroom. Six years ago, he had intimated just once that he wanted to make love to her. She, of course, told him they couldn't. Did he still hold a grudge? "There's always the TV."

His head tipped toward the corner of the room. "There's also a piano. I'd love to hear some more of your compositions. Would you play for me?"

She smiled, relieved that he didn't have a more intimate suggestion. "Of course. I'm glad they didn't return the piano to the music store yet."

"Who pays the moving and rental fees?"

"I suppose the music store, since they were one of the sponsors." She moved to the piano and started to play pieces that hadn't been included in the Chicago concert. Some were written shortly after he'd left for Paris when she was heartbroken. It brought back the memory of all those lonely nights when she had cried herself to sleep. Finally she was able to put her feelings into her music. In a way, it was like talking to a therapist. She'd been reliving her heartache through her music. It seemed to diminish the pain enough to go on without him.

He came up behind her and put his hands on her shoulders. He must have interpreted the pieces as she'd felt them when she'd written them. "I'm so sorry," he whispered.

Better late than never? She thought. "There were better times." She switched gears and played the more recent compositions, pieces that were written when she could look back on what they'd had together, the beautiful times, the memory of the love they'd shared.

A flutter of paper drew his attention to the door. He went over to pick up the paper, but thought better of it. She noticed what he was looking at and stopped playing.

"Another note?"

His head was bent so he could read the note without touching it. "I'm afraid so," he said on a sigh.

They both stood looking down at it until Laura went into the bedroom and returned wearing a pair of surgical gloves.

He had trouble keeping a straight face. "You have to be kidding. Do those come in Detective kit #1?"

She laughed. "Don't be cute. I always keep a supply on hand. I have often needed them for one reason or other while I'm away."

"May I ask what for?"

Her face turned only slightly pink. "I often had to wash out some underclothes when I was away from home. My hands don't do well in soapy water."

"Couldn't you have sent them to a laundry?"

"Oh, I did that once, and they brought them back practically ruined. They probably wash them with the regular laundry and they're too delicate for that. I won't take a chance on that happening again. It's easier to travel with my rubber gloves.

"Hmmm."

She looked up at him. "Hmmm what?"

"Nothing. I'm trying to picture your underwear." She was still shy and he enjoyed teasing her. "It must be pretty flimsy."

"Could we change the subject?" She picked up the note and read aloud. "It is with little pleasure I learned you are back. Are you daring me?"

"What does she want?" demanded Laura.

Charles put his arm around her shoulders. "Come on. Let's sit down." She nodded and followed him to the sofa. "You still think it's Carol?"

"Who else?"

"What happened to Ed Langston?"

She shrugged. "I can imagine that he might have had something to do with Fredrick's death; but why threaten me? I never did anything to him."

He took her hand in his. "Laura, it isn't what you or I think; it's whatever is in *his* mind. You know how some people are. They like to blame everyone for their troubles, everyone except themselves."

She took a deep breath. "I know that, but I hardly had anything to do with him."

"Could he have been jealous of your success?"

She closed her eyes, but the bitterness was apparent on her face. "I suppose a lot of people were. Carol, Ed and another music teacher." She tried to think of the name. "Cindy something. Cindy Meyer. That was it."

"What about Cindy? Who was she?"

"She fancied herself the world's most promising all-around musician and thought she should have had the honor of taking Fredrick's place after his death."

"She wasn't a student?"

"Oh, no. She was here when Fredrick took the job. Actually, he took *her* job. She was the department head. She was angry and she let everyone know. I think she secretly hoped that when her students found out, they'd stay with her out of loyalty, but they didn't. All but one transferred to Fredrick."

She looked into his eyes and saw what she thought was disapproval. Loyalty was high on his list of personality traits. "Why shouldn't they select the best teacher?" he asked. As an added thought, he said, "Was she good?"

"Yes. Cindy was good, but she wasn't great. Fredrick had his past career to back him up. She had teaching. That was all."

"Where is she now?"

"I don't know."

Charles opened the desk drawer to get the telephone directory. "Meyer." His finger followed the Ms down until he found Meyer.

"She's probably married by now or teaching someplace else."

"But she's not." He pointed to the page. "Cynthia Meyer. Could that be her?"

"Yes. Why are you so interested in her?"

"Don't you see? She could be another suspect. Who knew about her bad feelings?"

She chuckled. "The whole school. Cindy wasn't one to suffer in silence."

"That's another suspect for the chief."

"Why was she jealous of you?"

"I don't know. Maybe she fancied herself latching onto Fredrick."

"You mean romantically?"

She nodded. "The age was right. Also, she thought she might be able to influence him more than she actually could."

"What did he think of her?"

"I honestly don't know. He never talked about her. Well, just once when she told him he'd taken her job. She was angry, so she used her femininity on him and it didn't work. He could be quite aloof to anyone else's troubles. He saw only his own point of view. He was downright arrogant. I guess that comes from being a famous celebrity."

"Oh, I don't know," he said with a smile. "Fame didn't make you that way and I doubt that it ever would."

"You think you know me that well?"

"Yes." He leaned over, put his arms around her and kissed her lightly. He'd promised himself to see this whole thing through before he got more intimate, but it wasn't easy. The more he was with her, the more he realized that she'd grown into a woman even more fascinating than she'd been as a girl. She was everything a man could want. No wonder Scofield wanted her for himself, but he shuddered at the thought.

Had she not changed that much in six years? She didn't feel that he knew her the way she was now. Could it be that neither of them had changed in the important things, the things they loved about each other? She would have to give that some thought.

Friday morning, Charles heard a piece of paper being slipped under the door. Just as he got up to walk over and look, Laura came out of the bedroom.

"Good morning," she said cheerfully until she noticed where he was looking. Her face turned suddenly white. "Not again."

He would like to have saved her another threat, but it was too late. He went the rest of the way and bent over it to look at the paper.

"I'll get my gloves."

He held up his hand to stop her. "Don't bother. It's not a threat."

"Really?"

He smiled. "Really." He picked it up and read it. "It seems there's a musical at the college Friday and Saturday." He saw her obvious relief. He read out loud. "Words and music by Cynthia Meyer. I think we should go."

She smiled as she sat on the sofa, the bed already put together. "It will be fun." When was the last time she did something purely for fun? On tour, she spent every spare minute practicing or sleeping. Tours were hard on her. What was her excuse during the months she kept to herself? That was it. She kept to herself. After the photographers, fans and the media, she had to get away from it all and didn't even want to be seen in public.

He handed her the flyer. "It probably *will* be fun, but more than that, we may learn something about Miss Meyer and if we're lucky, we may see other people you knew back then. If so, you'll use your natural charm to get them talking."

She snapped her fingers. "I forgot my trench coat."

He laughed. The more time he spent with her, the more he realized how much he'd missed her serious side, her deep devotion and at times like this, her humor. He called himself every kind of fool for being so stupid that he'd believed Scofield six years ago. He thought he'd known her so well and yet, at the slightest provocation, he'd let her slip out of his fingers . . . No. He *gave* her away.

She studied his expression. His mind was elsewhere because there was anger in his eyes, in his stiff jaw. "A penny for your thoughts."

"Just remembering how stupid I was that night."

She didn't have to guess to which night he was referring. "Maybe we should agree to forget the past and start from this day forward."

"I don't think that's possible while we're delving in the past with Scofield's death. We're both forced to remember as much as possible that happened six years ago, and much more than we have so far."

"How do you mean?"

"When we go to the musical, I'm hoping we'll see people we knew before. We need to get as much information as possible."

"Brad and Craig are both doing that."

He nodded. "But people won't tell either of them as much as they'd tell us. We were one of them. Brad and Craig want something from them that they won't associate with us. They probably think they're being interrogated."

"With Craig, they are. I hope we can find out something that will help him."

"We can hope." He went to her and lifted her chin with his forefinger. "I know I said we should go slowly, even if it's difficult; but until the investigation is over, let's agree to be friends and no more." She started to speak, but he went on. "As hard as it is to keep my hands off you, I think it's vital to table that until later. We might even learn something from it."

"Like what?" she asked.

"Six years ago, we never gave ourselves time to really know each other. I've already learned a lot. You've grown into a woman who is not just the talented girl I loved, but a sensitive, caring woman whose values are commendable and a woman I want to know as well as I know myself."

She blushed. "That's quite a speech. Are you sure I'm that woman?"

"I'm very sure." He leaned over and kissed her cheek. "Don't worry. That was a platonic kiss, one friend to another."

She nodded. She couldn't say she wasn't disappointed, but she knew he was acting wisely and she found that she loved him for it. Well, if he could be just friends for the sake of the investigation, so could she.

"Don't forget," he added as if he could read her thoughts, "I'm concerned about your safety. If I were to get distracted by my feelings," he shuddered, "I'd never forgive myself if anything happened to you."

"You don't think I can take care of myself?"

"For the most part, I suppose you can, but didn't you tell me how the SUV tried to run you down, and how close it came to doing just that?"

She smiled sheepishly because she knew what she was going to say would sound stupid, but she couldn't help saying it. "But it *did* miss me. Don't forget that."

He looked at her with a sideways glance that said *I won't even answer that.* She had seen that look may times when they were young.

"I used to call that your *don't-say-another-word* look.

The phone rang as he laughed.

"Hello," Laura answered.

"Laura. It's Brad. Have you had breakfast?"

"Not yet. We were just headed for the coffee shop. Would you like to join us?" She looked at Charles for approval.

"How about walking a block down to the Copper Kettle? I want to see you, but I want people to think it's by accident. I'll be there in about two minutes. I'll sit at a table in the back. When you see me, come over to say hello and I'll invite you to join me. What do you think?"

Laura held her hand over the phone and asked Charles. He nodded. "We'll be there shortly."

Charles put the flyer into his pocket. "What do you suppose he wants?"

"He didn't say, but maybe he was able to catch Alvin Freeman."

"Let's hope he learned something new."

He checked the hall and nodded that it was empty so they could leave together. "Isn't this behavior a bit cloak and dagger?" he whispered.

"Very definitely."

Five minutes later they entered the Copper Kettle, a quaint cafe with red and white checkered tablecloths. An assortment of kettles rested on shelves on two walls.

"Mr. Nielson," said Laura approaching his table. "How nice to see you again. Have you met Charles Templeton?" She made sure her voice was strong enough for anyone to hear if they were listening.

Brad shook hands with Charles and asked them to join him. They were at a table in the rear where they couldn't be heard. Even so, they spoke softly.

Laura looked around before speaking. "Have you talked to Alvin?"

Brad shook his head. "I'm sure he's avoiding me and I don't like it one bit. I'm getting the feeling he has something to hide."

Charles grinned. "It looks like we have a few suspects for what happened six years ago, but I'm more interested in the threats Laura's been getting." He carefully took the note out of his pocket and held it with two fingers on the very edge to show it to Brad.

"Another one?" Rather than touch the paper, he simply read it.

She nodded. "Like the other one, only this one says, *are you daring me?*"

Brad sighed. "Be careful. You *are* staying with her, aren't you, Templeton?"

"Absolutely. The bathroom and bedroom are the only places she's alone."

Brad was thoughtful. "I don't think it's wise to--"

"She's in a suite. I'm on the sofa bed."

He made a grunting noise. "Good." The waitress came to take their orders. When she left, she returned with coffee and said the food would be up shortly.

"Brad, we've come up with some suspects."

"For the threats?"

"For the. . . " she looked around, "death," she whispered..

He knew she meant Scofield's death. "Interesting. Who?"

"Ed Langston, for one."

"And," offered Charles, "Cynthia Meyer."

Brad frowned. "Who?"

Charles went on. "Scofield took her job when he was hired. She was angry."

"I'll bet."

"After he died, she wanted her title back and didn't get it. Laura also wonders if she didn't fancy herself as the future Mrs. Scofield."

Brad thought about it. "Good work, you two."

Laura took a sip of coffee. "We plan on doing more if we can. We're going to the musical tonight at the college."

"What do you hope to gain there?"

"Entertainment, of course." She needed to use a little humor, but noticed that Brad wasn't laughing. She took a deep breath. Brad had no sense of humor. "Charles thought it was a good place to make contact with people who were here six years ago."

"That's good thinking. You will probably know some of the people. Your insight is invaluable, you know."

The waitress brought their food, cutting short Laura's feeling of pride.

Brad put syrup on his pancakes. "I would like to surprise Al Freeman with a visit. He should be back in town tomorrow. How about coming with me to question him?"

"Sure," she answered, "but make sure he'll be there."

"If not, I'll ask the chief to do it. Would Freeman dare avoid the police?"

Laura laughed. "I didn't know him well, but I think he'd be afraid to look guilty."

"He can refuse me, but not the police. Does Craig know what you dug up?"

"Not yet. I was going to call him after breakfast. We're not to go to the station."

Brad nodded. "No point in letting everyone know we're all working together. That's why I suggested meeting here."

"I'm glad you did."

"Will you keep me informed on what you find out tonight at the musical?"

"Of course, if there's anything to report."

Charles looked from one to the other. "You have to have faith. I'm quite sure we'll learn something new."

Brad was already thinking ahead to what his next move would be. "Then you'll come with me if I can pinpoint where Al is?"

She looked at Charles for approval. "By all means."

"You did say he doesn't live in Webster City, didn't you?" asked Charles.

"He lives in Dalton."

Charles nodded. "That's not too far."

"But far enough to avoid anyone seeing us and putting two and two together. Let's try for tomorrow morning say at about ten?"

"If you call him to make sure he'll be there, won't you be tipping your hand?"

"I've already established that I'm doing an article on Scofield's life. Even so, I've been calling under an assumed name just in case."

Charles sighed. "More cloak and dagger stuff."

They all laughed, but each one knew it wasn't a laughing matter. "I'll meet you here at ten? We'll take my car from here."

"Won't Alvin recognize your car?" asked Charles.

"Good point. We'll take your car. See you in the morning."

Chapter 8

The college theater was crowded, which was normal for opening night. Everyone wanted to be the first to see it. Charles and Laura took their seats in the fifth row. It was one of the best seats, making Charles wonder if the woman who sold the tickets knew Laura. How else would they get such good seats when buying the tickets last minute? He assumed that they always kept a few special seats open for celebrities or well known contributors to the college fund. No doubt, Laura qualified for both.

From somewhere behind them, they heard a woman saying, "Excuse me, please. Excuse me, would you let me through, please? Thank you."

Just as Laura was sitting down, she heard her name.

"Laura? Laura Westlund?" The woman was right behind Charles.

Laura looked at the woman. It took her a minute to put a name to the face she had seen so often. "Melissa?"

"You remembered."

Laura smiled. "Of course. How could I forget?" She noticed the well-lined face which had once been what they called a peaches and cream complexion. Would six years really do that? She'd have to take a very close look in the mirror when she got back to the hotel. "Melissa, this is Charles Templeton. Charles, meet Melissa McAllister." She turned to Melissa. "I don't believe he was here when you were. Didn't you start when I was in my last year?"

"Yes." She looked at Charles. "It's nice to meet you." She looked as if she were trying to remember something. Her eyes lit up. "Templeton? *The* Charles Templeton?"

He bowed his head slightly. "I'm afraid so." They shook hands.

"How wonderful. I just bought one of your paintings in Chicago, *The Louvre*. It's gorgeous." He opened his mouth to comment, but she went right on talking. "I missed the showing, but I managed to get there the next day. How wonderful. I'm so excited." She turned back to Laura and spoke softly. "I see you didn't let him get away after all."

Charles glanced at Laura, wondering what she meant.

"What are you doing here, Melissa? I thought you were from Colorado."

"I was, but they offered me the position of Department Head. I couldn't refuse."

"So they passed Cindy up again?"

Melissa stared at Laura. "You didn't hear what happened?"

"Obviously not. What?"

"Cindy told anyone who'd listen that you stole Fredrick away from her."

"Why on earth would she do that? I told her I wasn't interested and never was."

"It might not have had anything to do with you."

"How could it not?" Laura looked around and realized she was speaking way too loud. She didn't want to draw attention to herself.

"Cindy wanted to marry him. Well, she wanted more than that, but she made such a fuss about it, they all but fired her. She was as angry as a person can get. I can't tell you how terrible it was. We were all glad you were well away from here. She might have tried to harm you."

"Really?" Laura's mind flew to the threats and the SUV incident, not to mention the verbal threat Carol made. Craig's thinking wasn't far off. It could be Cindy, but could they prove it? She would have to be questioned about where she was at the times of his death and at the times she received the threats. Could they prove that Cindy killed Fredrick? Then what about Carol? This was getting confusing.

The lights flickered as a signal for people to find their seats.

"Can we talk after the play?" asked Melissa.

Laura looked to Charles for his approval. "Let's meet in the lobby."

They agreed before Melissa moved to her seat two rows back.

When the curtain rose, the scene was a luxury apartment. The orchestra started and the audience was expectantly quiet. When the overture was done a girl came from the side of the stage singing *This Is A City*. Laura stiffened, glanced at Charles and grabbed his arm.

He looked at her. Even in the darkness he could see the stricken look on her face. "What's the matter?"

She shook her head and whispered in his ear. "I wrote that song." She couldn't believe what she heard. As the performance went on, she realized it wasn't the only song she wrote. "That's my musical, Charles."

His other hand reached over to rest on her arm. He whispered in her ear. "We'll deal with this after the performance."

How could Cindy claim that she had written it? She tried to calm down. She listened carefully to each and every word. She hadn't written the overture, but she did write *This Is A City*, and the girl singing it did the exact movements she had written into the script. She also wrote the dialog.

"I like it," said Charles with a twinkle in his eye.

That's all she needed to relax. So even if she wasn't getting credit for it, it should be fun to see her musical performed onstage. She had a million questions, but tabled them for now. Charles was right. There was nothing they could do right now.

She had such mixed emotions. She was thrilled the way the students performed her musical; but she couldn't deny her anger and hurt. What had Cindy been thinking? Did she think she could get away with claiming that she wrote it? Laura had all the proof she needed in her computer. She had written it during her third year here. How did Cindy get hold of it? She had to hand in the whole thing, words and music to get a grade, but it was returned to her. Could Fredrick have made a copy? Why would he? He'd graded the music, Professor Simpson the text. Did he still teach here? Too many questions.

Charles reached over and took her hand in his. He could imagine how she must feel. If someone took one of his paintings and signed their own name under it, he would be furious. Laura had worked for almost a year on this. He smiled to himself. Not only was the music really good, but the whole performance was something he wouldn't have wanted to miss. When he heard *Will the Phone Ring*, he leaned over and whispered, "I remember this one." He smiled and squeezed her hand.

His smile always did make her feel special. It meant even more now. The song ended and the curtain came down for the intermission. He stood up. "Let's stretch our legs. Would you like something to drink?"

She nodded and they followed the line heading for the beverage table that had been set up in the lobby. They hadn't been there for a minute when someone grabbed Laura's arm. It was Melissa.

"How can she do that?" she asked Laura.

"Do what?"

"You wrote that, Laura. I heard Professor Simpson read sections of it to his class. He used it as an example of writing good dialog." Laura had shrugged, but Melissa wouldn't drop the subject. "Aren't you going to do something about it?"

Laura leaned closer so she wouldn't be heard. "I'm not sure what, though."

"Well," she huffed, "I can think of at least four or five students who'd remember. A couple of them still live around here. The nerve of that woman! I'm going to expose her for what she is."

Laura didn't want a fuss right now. That would spoil everything they came here to do. She shot a quick glance at Charles. He seemed to read her thoughts.

"Why don't we talk afterwards," he suggested.

"I can't just let this slide. As Department Head, I'm responsible for the whole department. She's part of it."

Charles cringed. She was speaking much too loud. "Let's not make waves where everyone can hear us. We'll discuss it over coffee at the Meeting Place?"

Melissa agreed to meet them shortly after the performance.

"Save us a table. We have to talk to a couple people before we leave."

"Fine."

The lights flashed a warning and they headed back for their seats.

During the rest of the performance, Charles threw glances of admiration at Laura. He felt a kind of pride that he'd never felt before. Didn't he know she was this talented six years ago? Had Scofield's infatuation with her spoiled that? Again, he felt ashamed for believing him.

The lights came on and people stood up to walk out to the lobby where the performers would greet them along with Cynthia, who would, or at least *should* be shocked to see Laura. Charles was counting on it, wondering what she would say.

Having sat so far down front, it took almost fifteen minutes to reach the lobby. Once there, Laura and Charles congratulated the cast and got to Cindy as she was finishing a conversation with someone. As she turned to greet them, her face turned white and she looked around for an escape, but that was impossible. She straightened her shoulders and looked Laura directly in her eyes. "Did you enjoy the performance?" she asked in a steely voice.

"I would have enjoyed it more," said Charles, "if we'd been told who really wrote that musical."

Cindy stiffened, looked around and quickly said, "Excuse me. I have to check backstage."

Charles smiled a cold smile. "Don't worry, we'll come with you."

"I'm afraid you--"

"No problem," he said as he put his hand under her elbow and led her backstage with Laura following.

Laura hadn't wanted to talk about this right now. She didn't know what she wanted to say to Cindy. She was really angry at her, but seeing her very own musical so well performed was an experience she never thought she'd have. She was thankful for that, but Cindy had done wrong when she claimed to have written it.

By the time they got back stage, one worker was moving the set around, getting it ready for tomorrow's performance. Charles dropped his hand from Cindy's arm as she went on ahead. She didn't notice that they were still following. When she heard footsteps behind her, she turned around and sighed as she saw them.

"What do you want?" she asked belligerently.

Laura stood very still, just looking at her pale face. "I think you know."

"Know what?" She tried to sound innocent.

Charles couldn't believe this woman. "You know. The musical?" He turned his head up and waited to hear what she'd say.

"What about it?"

Charles narrowed his eyes. "Let's not play games. You are in trouble, Miss Meyer."

She was trembling, but still claiming innocence. "I don't know what you mean."

"Cindy, we both know you didn't write that."

"I beg your pardon. Who else would have written it?"

"Let's not do this." Laura said. "You know very well that I wrote that musical."

Cindy nervously looked at Charles. "Is that what she told you?" She turned to Laura. "What proof do you have?"

Charles stepped in. "She has proof."

"Did you think I wouldn't have kept my script? I also have it in my computer."

"And the music?" she squeaked out.

"And the music," said Laura firmly, becoming angrier with each evasive comment Cindy made.

Cindy's body slumped. She would not be able to save herself, but she was unable to say a word until another thought struck her. "You could have copied it," she accused.

"I'm afraid not. Cindy. I received my *original* back. *You* must have copied it."

She shook her head. "No. I didn't." Her shoulders slumped. "I found the script in the bottom drawer in Professor Scofield's office. I liked it so I wrote the overture."

"Why would Fredrick make copies?"

"Because he was going to claim it was his."

Laura frowned, unsure of what she was about to say. "I doubt that very much."

"Doubt it all you want, but I just did what he intended to do. Besides, I saw a few others in that file drawer. They were all complete musicals, words and music. None of them had names on them. Freddie had made some red marks in some of them where he wanted changes."

"I didn't detect any changes."

"Oh," Cindy said sarcastically. "He'd never change a note of *your* music."

Laura thought back. Fredrick had asked them not to put names on them, but a number. He'd appointed one student to assign numbers and was asked to keep the list so Fredrick wouldn't know which number belonged to which student. When it was time to hand them back, they would claim their musical by number. "I remember Fredrick saying he didn't want to be swayed by knowing the composer of the script, but would grade them only on their merits." She remembered that when they received their manuscripts back, they were able to put their names at the top before handing the dialogue script in to the drama department. Evidently, they felt able to be impartial in spite of knowing who wrote what.

Cindy was desperate. "Then you have no proof. Your name isn't on it."

Charles had run out of patience. "Let's go, Laura. We'll contact a lawyer."

"No!" cried Cindy. She waited for a moment, trying desperately to think of something. "What do you want from me?"

Charles again broke in. "A public apology is the first thing."

Laura looked at Charles. He was right, but there had to be more to it than that. Should they see a lawyer? What would they gain? "Let's make that a first step."

Cindy was at the point of tears. "I'll be fired."

"Maybe you should have thought of that before." Charles took Laura's arm and led her to the steps that took them out of the auditorium. A few people were still milling around the lobby. They'd left Cindy stunned.

Laura shook her head. "What a mess."

"A mess of her own making."

"True, but how will this affect the college?"

Charles considered that question. He hadn't thought of that. It definitely would bring bad publicity. "No doubt, it will cause trouble."

"Can't we avoid that?" she asked. "I love this college. I don't want to publicize this. It could ruin the college. All because of one woman. Well, one woman and Fredrick, but the college shouldn't suffer for it."

"True. A scandal never does any good."

As they approached the lobby, Laura whispered, "Let's think it over."

"Let her suffer for a while." They walked to the front door where several people were gathered.

"Laura Westlund." A man was walking toward them with an outstretched hand.

Laura shook his hand. He looked familiar, but she couldn't put a name to the face.

"You may not remember me. Carl Hahn."

"Of course, Carl." She turned to Charles. "You remember Carl, don't you?"

Charles grinned. "How could I forget?"

The men shook hands and stood eye to eye. Laura had a feeling they had known each other quite well.

Carl finally grinned. "Do you always have to spoil my chances with her?" His words were good natured.

Charles shrugged. "Don't look at me. I've been in Paris for six years."

"I've been at UCLA."

"I take it you were good friends," Laura observed.

Carl cringed. "I-ah wouldn't exactly say that. Chuck and I wanted to date the same girl." He looked at Charles. "What happened that took you to Paris?"

"It's a long story. What took you to UCLA?"

"When Scofield told me he was going to marry Laura, I gave up any hope of dating her. I was offered a position at UCLA, and," he shrugged, "I like warm weather."

"So Scofield told you, too."

He looked at Laura. "You didn't marry him?"

"That pompous--" She was so angry, she could hardly speak. "You both must have left right away."

They both nodded.

Charles sighed heavily. "I don't believe this. Carl and I constantly argued, but I saw you first, and I dated you first, so I claimed you."

She looked at Carl. "What could I do? He did date you and as much as I wanted to, I couldn't compete with him." He grimaced and turned to Charles. "If I'd known you left, I could have--"

"Don't even think it. You believed Scofield just as much as I did."

"But how could you?"

"How could *you*?"

Laura moved so she was standing between them. "That's enough. It looks like Fredrick spoiled all of our lives."

Charles smiled tenderly and put his arm around Laura. "I wouldn't say that."

Carl ginned and nodded. "So that's the way it is."

"Yup. That's the way it is." Charles turned serious. "How is UCLA? Any hotshot concert pianists down there?"

"As a matter of fact," he held up his left hand that was adorned with a wedding ring, "there is. Her name is Heather, and we're having our first baby in a week or so."

They both congratulated him.

Laura was curious. "Then why are you here? Shouldn't you be there with her?"

"My plane leaves at eleven tonight. She assures me that she won't go into labor until I'm home. I had to be here today to interview a senior we're very interested in having at UCLA. I caught the musical while I waited out the evening."

Charles patted Carl's shoulder. "Best of luck to you."

"And you, too," he answered. Carl's curiosity got the better of him. "What about Scofield? Did he actually ask you to marry him?"

"You didn't hear that he died?" she asked.

"Died? From what?"

"They labeled it suicide because there was no evidence to prove otherwise, but Chief Thomas is considering reopening the case."

"What was the cause of death?"

"Overdose of sleeping pills," she answered.

Charles added. "Besides having been drinking heavily."

Carl shook his head. "No way. Scofield wouldn't touch a drop of alcohol. The man wouldn't even eat food that was cooked with wine."

"Are you sure?" asked Laura. It struck Laura and Charles as very odd, to say the least. Would that change Craig's mind? It sounded more and more like murder to them.

"Absolutely. I sat next to him at a dinner when they served veal in wine sauce. He refused it and asked for a piece of veal without the sauce. He said he had a very strict upbringing."

They continued discussing Scofield's death until Carl's cell phone rang. "Excuse me." He went to the corner of the lobby to answer. When he returned, he tucked the cell phone in his pocket. "It looks like the boy I interviewed is going to come to UCLA to look it over. It's promising."

"What are you two doing here? Are you part of the faculty?"

Charles shook his head and told Carl about Scofield's death and the threats.

"Were the threats connected to Scofield's death?"

He shrugged. "We want answers."

"Do you know who might have killed Scofield?"

Laura answered. "There are a few people with motives, Carol Harding, Cindy Meyer, Ed Langston and possibly Alvin Freeman."

Carl's eyes narrowed to slits. "Now that one I can believe. I never saw a guy with criminal behavior quite like him, but drugs can do that." He recalled another fact. "He was a model student the first couple months and then . . . he changed. Just like that." He snapped his fingers.

"Drugs?"

"Anything he could get his hands on. He came to his lesson as high as a kite one day. Scofield knew the score. They argued and Al left in a fit of anger. He threatened Scofield, but I can't remember exactly what he said. It's been years."

"You witnessed it?"

"Darn right. It was the next day that Scofield told me about his proposal. His *phony* proposal. I left the next day."

Charles cringed. "So did I."

His head snapped toward Charles. He had trouble believing that Scofield had fooled both of them. "Why didn't you question Freeman?"

"Actually," said Laura, "Chief Thomas and Brad Nielson have tried to talk to him, but he's been evading them."

"Nielson? Should I know him?"

Laura shook her head. "He's a reporter. He said he moved here about five years ago, after the fact, but he's interested."

Carl looked at his watch. "I'd better leave before I miss my plane." He shook hands with Charles. "It's been nice seeing you two. I take it that you're together again."

Charles grinned. "It's not going to break your heart this time?"

"Absolutely not." He grinned and pointed to his wedding ring. "I only hope you'll be half as happy as Heather and I are."

He glanced at Laura, "I'm certainly trying."

Carl hugged Laura. "You deserve to be happy. He's a good man." He backed off and with a wave of his hand, he left.

As they watched him leave, Charles put his arm around Laura. "This gets more interesting every day."

She nodded. "Another suspect. Do you believe it?"

After talking to a few more people, they went back to the hotel. Laura said she'd call Brad right away, but would wait until morning to call Craig. His day started so early, she didn't want to wake him for something he wouldn't pursue until tomorrow anyway.

Morning came quickly. "Where did you say we were meeting them?"

"Craig wants to be seen by as few people as possible. It's called the Pump House five miles out of town."

"The way we see someone everywhere we go, we might just as well meet them at the police station."

"Let's just hope nobody will notice us. I'd think only those involved in the threats or in Fredrick's death would think anything of seeing us together. Actually, we'll be in a small meeting room at the back of the restaurant."

"It'll be interesting to compare notes with them."

Charles was putting the sofa bed together when Laura came into the room.

"I'm sorry you have to sleep on that imitation mattress."

He laughed. "I haven't heard you invite me to join you in there." His head nodded toward the bedroom.

She laughed. "And you won't. I've matured, but my morals haven't changed."

He stood directly in front of her and put his hands on her shoulders. "I'm glad."

Her eyes opened wide. "You are?"

"Yes. Your innocence was one of the things I loved about you; but you knew where to draw the line."

"I seem to remember that you weren't always so glad," she teased.

He shrugged. "That was youth . . . and hormones."

They arrived at the Pump House and parked in the lot behind the building. Charles looked around. "I don't see the police car."

"I don't suppose he'll be driving it here. That would be like advertising."

"You're right. What makes you so smart?"

She shrugged. "I guess I never used to consider anything obvious without consciously thinking about it. Do you suppose it's fear?"

He reached over and put his arm around her shoulders, pulling her closer to him.

"I think you've had too many threats and the thought that Scofield was murdered doesn't help. I'm proud of you, Laura. Most women would have run from a situation like this. You're facing it head on. I only hope you won't take chances."

She chuckled. "How can I? I'm not alone for a second unless I'm sleeping or in the bathroom."

Charles suddenly wondered if his protective attitude bothered her. "I'm sorry if you're uncomfortable with it, but I don't want to see anything happen to you. I just found you again, and I don't intend to let anything happen to you. It's a purely selfish thing."

"You have such a nice way of explaining it. How can I object?"

"You could blame me for being selfish."

"Hardly."

Charles looked at the car driving into the lot. "And this would be a nice time to kiss you, but we have company." His head leaned toward the car driving in.

Craig got out of his wife's car and walked into the building without looking at them. "He's not advertising that we're meeting him here."

He nodded. "Cloak and dagger all the way." He grinned and waited until Craig was in the building before opening his door. He helped Laura out of the car and was almost at the door when they saw Brad enter the lot. He parked his car while they went inside. They'd do the same as Craig had done.

Before they could ask any questions, the hostess looked around, pointed to a door in the back and nodded that they should go on in. There was only one table with three people in the front of the building, and they were so engrossed in their conversation, it was doubtful that they'd even seen the couple enter.

They found Craig at a blackboard, erasing what had been written.

Charles raised an eyebrow. "Is this a common meeting place or do you provide your own props?"

Craig stopped long enough to greet them. When Brad entered, he greeted him as well and told them to take a seat. He wrote *Suspects* on the board. "I thought we'd compare notes and see where we stand. If there's probable cause, I'll reopen the case and charge Carol Harding."

"That might be a bit premature," said Laura.

"How so?"

Laura let Charles explain. "I'm afraid we have a couple more suspects."

Craig didn't look pleased. He was sure he had enough evidence to arrest Carol. "Let's hear it."

"Well," said Laura, "Cynthia Meyer is the teacher whose job Fredrick took. She was angry. When he died, she expected to get her title back, but they bypassed her and chose Melissa McAllister." She watched him for a reaction and was disappointed when he gave no sign of understanding. "It's also been said that she thought Fredrick would propose to her."

That got a reaction. "That man must have had some effect on women."

"Not on this one," she said, her finger jabbing her chest. "And, of course, you know about Ed Langston."

"Who is he?" asked Brad.

Craig answered. "The troublesome nephew of Professor Standish."

Laura's head snapped up as she searched Craig's eyes. She saw that he was serious. "Are you saying that Ed Langston is Professor Standish's nephew?"

"You didn't know?"

"I never associated *Ed* with *Eduardo*. Why did I never know that?"

"Eduardo didn't want it known that his uncle was on the faculty." Craig turned toward her. "You remember the day Professor Standish came in to see me."

"Yes, but Ed Langston is the professor's nephew Eduardo?" she repeated.

Craig got up and wrote the two names on the board with their motives. "All right then," he said on a sigh, knowing that this was more complicated than he'd thought.

"Not so fast." Brad took out his notebook. "It seems that Stuart Engleman hated Scofield's guts. He studied here for only two years and he tangled with Scofield every time they saw each other. It was a mutual hate thing, but nobody seems to know just what caused the ill feelings."

"Then," offered Charles, "there's Alvin Freeman."

Brad apologized. "I can't get him to sit still long enough to interview him."

"We learned an interesting bit of information about him." Laura looked at Brad squarely. "He's been on drugs. I don't know if he still is, but when he was studying with Fredrick, they had a big fight. He was heard threatening Fredrick."

"How?"

Charles shook his head. "Our source witnessed the anger and the threat, but he said it was years ago. He couldn't remember his words."

Craig jotted the name on the board. "Who is the source?"

"Carl Hahn. H a h n. He teaches at UCLA so it should be easy to get hold of him."

"Good work."

From there, they discussed several possibilities and reasons for their suspicions. They agreed that each one had motive for the threats and/or the possible murder.

"The difficult task is to get hard evidence. After all, Scofield had been drinking--"

Charles shook his head. "Scofield didn't drink."

"What?" snapped Craig. "How do you know?"

"Carl Hahn told us tonight. He knew for a fact that Scofield never touched a drop of alcohol. Come to think of it, I vaguely remember his saying that God didn't intend for man to abuse his body with alcohol or drugs. He was genuinely upset."

Laura was confused. "Why didn't you mention that before?"

He shook his head. "I don't know. It just didn't strike me when you told me about his death. All that registered was *sleeping pills*."

"If Scofield didn't touch alcohol," said Craig, "that automatically suggests homicide. I wonder why nobody offered that information before."

Brad offered the answer. "Maybe the ones who heard about it didn't know. Maybe the ones who knew hadn't heard the details of his death. Or maybe, one in particular had a good reason not to offer that information."

Craig stared at the board. His forefinger and thumb on his chin. "What a revolting development this turned out to be. One death, too many suspects, and six years late."

He turned to the blackboard again. "All right. From the beginning." He wrote Carol Harding's name on the board under *suspects*. "Motive?"

Laura was first. "Carol thought she should have received the award Fredrick gave to me. She also thought she should have been chosen for the concert tour."

Craig nodded.

Brad checked his notes. "She fancied herself in love with Scofield. She was angry with him, and she resented Laura for being his choice for the award."

"So Carol had motive to kill Scofield as revenge. She resented Laura, so could have been responsible for at least one, if not all, of the threats. She has a dark green SUV, so could have tried to run Laura down." He looked all around, but nobody had anything more to contribute. "So--"

"Let's not forget," Laura interrupted, "that the threats could have been written by two different people. They were not the same. Carol also verbally threatened me, but we have to consider that the timing of some of the threats doesn't seem logical."

Craig nodded. "Agreed. Now," he looked at Laura and Charles, "you said Cindy Meyer was a possible suspect."

Charles nodded. "Scofield took her job as department head when they first hired him. When he died, she expected her job title back, but they overlooked her and chose Melissa McAllister. We also think she had feelings for Scofield, maybe hoped to marry him. She stole Laura's musical, wrote an overture for it and claimed she wrote it, words and music. What better motive to want her gone?"

Brad couldn't believe anyone would stoop so low. "That's a lot of gall. How did she expect to get by with it?"

"She obviously didn't expect me to attend the performance."

Craig jotted key words for motives. He wrote the next name. "Ed Langston."

Laura spoke up. "Ed was Fredrick's most promising student for about two months. Ed evidently changed and Fredrick wasn't so eager about Ed's talent. Something happened and Fredrick refused to teach him. The next semester, he made Miss Compton teach him. Ed was furious with him for that or for something else. He had a big argument with him, using foul language and calling him awful names. He stormed out saying, "I'll get you for this, Scofield.' He slammed the door and left."

Craig was thoughtful. "Standish always said he was a problem." Craig waited for further comments and finally wrote another name. "Alvin Harding."

"So far, nothing," said Brad.

"Except," said Charles holding up his hand, "that Alvin was on drugs, had an argument with Scofield and threatened him." He added, "Carl Hahn, witness."

"What kind of a college is this? Is it that easy to get drugs?"

Brad threw up his hands. "Like any other college, or high school, for that matter. If there's a demand for drugs, there will be someone all too happy to supply them."

"And make a tidy sum doing it." Craig waited for further comments. When there were none, he wrote that information on the board. "Anyone else?"

Brad chuckled. "Isn't that enough?"

"Quite." Craig took out a digital camera, snapped a picture of the blackboard and erased the information he'd written. "I'll call when I have anything more to report. You do the same. This seems to be a good place to meet, so we'll plan to meet here when anything else comes up. We'll use off hours when there isn't a crowd. Call me. Let me go out first. Give it a couple minutes and Brad, go next. Good work, people."

Chapter 9

After church on Sunday, Charles and Laura were recapping the information about the suspects. "What a mess," he said.

"Yes. I'm sure that if we tried, we'd find a few more people who disliked Fredrick." Laura thought back. If only Brad had been able to question Alvin. He was in town Saturday night, but was not at home and not available.

"You know, I had the impression that Scofield was the celebrity who could draw students like flies. I thought he was well liked."

"He was at first, but I'm sure the circumstances grated on him. He could no longer do what he felt God chose him to do. He mentioned not being able to sleep. He was always tired and irritable."

"You mean not being able to continue his concerts?"

She nodded. "I suppose so. He had become judgmental and critical, quite different from the way he was when he first came here. I suppose self pity caused part of that." She sighed. "As a result, he made a lot of enemies. I didn't notice it until probably the last three months before his death. Some of his students were talking behind his back."

"Why didn't you mention it to the Dean of Women?"

Laura had a sad smile. "I thought it was temporary, that he would realize what was happening and would wake up and realize that his life wasn't over. It was such a good opportunity to help students realize their goals. More than that, he helped them see that they were worthy of setting goals. I know he made me realize I could do more than teach piano lessons."

Charles shook his head. "That's too bad. Someone with so much power to help, and he threw it all away with self pity."

"That's about it."

"So did you ever fancy yourself in his future?" he asked carefully.

"Need you ask?"

He chuckled. "No." His cell phone rang. Just as he answered it, the telephone in the suite rang.

Charles covered the phone with his hand. "I'll go across the hall to take this There's a problem at the gallery. Give me half an hour or so."

She nodded and watched him leave as she answered the phone. "Hello."

"Laura, it's Brad. I want to make a surprise visit to Al, no warning. Do you have time to go with me?"

"When?"

"Forty-five minutes or so?"

"Charles should be done with his call by then. I'll run out to the car and get my notes. We'll meet you at the Pump House, hopefully no longer than forty-five minutes from now. If there's a change, I'll catch you on your cell phone." Something in her notes had bothered her. She needed to go over them before the interview.

"Good enough. See you then." He disconnected.

Laura put on her jacket. She'd run out, get her notes, then knock on the door across the hall and inform Charles of the plans. She'd look over the notes until Charles was done.

Laura walked down the stairs to the lobby. The desk clerk asked if she needed anything. She thanked him, telling him she was just running out to get something from the car. Maybe she should go out the back door that opened to the parking lot. If anyone was watching, they'd expect her to leave through the front door. She was proud of herself for thinking of it. This cloak and dagger stuff was rubbing off on her. As she approached the door, she realized it was solid metal. The front door was glass and one could see out front. She'd have to go with her instinct and not worry about anyone watching her. When she was outside, she'd wait by the door for a moment to look around the area. If anyone was there, she'd see them.

She berated herself for being so paranoid. It didn't make sense that someone would watch the back of the building. Besides, it was broad daylight. Would anyone even think of doing anything that could be seen from windows or people going to their cars?

She opened the door cautiously and stuck her head out to look around. After assuring herself that nobody was there, she stepped out and looked around again. She then walked past the dumpster next to the building. She was about to run for her car when an arm suddenly gripped her neck from behind. How could she have missed seeing someone? The dumpster! How could she be so stupid? She tried to jar herself loose.

"Don't even think about it," said a very hoarse woman's voice. Or was it a man's voice, trying to sound like a woman? "We're going to walk to that Toyota at the end of the driveway. I'm going to put my arm around you like we're just friends walking."

Whoever it was had bent her arm behind her and had disabled her. "Answer me."

The arm around her neck was choking her. She couldn't breathe or utter a word and was about to lose consciousness. What did this person want? Who could it be? What if she didn't do as she was told? Fear was getting the best of her. What would happen if she fainted? Surely, a woman couldn't pick her up and carry her. It had to be a man, she reasoned, but she could be wrong. No matter how deserted the parking lot looked, he couldn't risk being seen. If she didn't cooperate, what would he do? No way would she willingly get in that car. If he wanted something from her, he wouldn't kill her. Would he? She was more frightened than she had ever been in her life.

Charles finished his call and went back to the suite, but the door was locked. He knocked, but there was no answer. He dialed her number with his cell phone, but there was no answer. He ran down the steps to the lobby.

He tried to sound normal, but couldn't. "Have you seen Miss Westlund?"

"I believe she went out back to get something from her car."

"Thanks." Charles should have been relieved, but he gave in to the panic that made him rush to the back door. Why would she go out to the car by herself? She knew better. He opened the door and stormed out, but froze when he saw Laura lying on the pavement a few feet from the door. As he ran to her, he was aware of a car door slamming. He saw that the driver wore a hat and had a mustache.

"Laura," he said kneeling down beside her. Her face was snow white against the black pavement.

"I'm all right." Her voice was hoarse and weak, but she was talking.

"What happened?"

"Someone grabbed me." She pointed toward the dumpster. When she'd turned her head, he saw blood on her cheek. He took her chin and held her face so he could examine it more closely.

"Laura, you're bleeding." He took out a clean handkerchief and blotted the blood. There was a scrape along the left side of her face with a scratch about two inches long that was oozing blood. It didn't appear to be deep so there would be no need for stitches, but she wasn't going to be happy when she looked in a mirror. His hands balled into fists as he looked around. Nobody was in sight.

"Man or woman?"

"I don't know? It could have been either."

"Can you stand?" He helped her up and took her weight once she was standing. "What made you--"

"Please don't yell, Charles."

He pulled her close. "Sorry, but it was foolish."

"I know that now."

"What were you doing out here?"

"I needed my notes from the car. We have to meet Brad at the Pump House."

"That may not happen. Let's get you inside and call the chief."

"We'll go in and get our things. You can call on the way to the Pump House."

Charles didn't say anything. He knew Laura would do what she had to, so why upset her even more? They were by the elevator when Laura caught a glimpse of herself in the mirror. "Oh, no."

"Wait until we get to the room. You can put a cold compress on it for a minute. In fact, if you're determined that to meet Brad, take it in the car with you. It will keep the swelling down and hopefully take care of some of the red."

"I look awful, Charles." She was close to tears.

He squeezed her shoulder. "It's only temporary. Not even the bruises can mar your beauty." The elevator doors opened and they stepped inside.

She tried to smile, but it hurt. "Only you would say that."

"That's good. That means I don't have any competition."

Her mouth formed a pout. "You don't have to make me feel better, you know."

"Is it okay if I make *me* feel better? Laura, it could have been a lot worse. What did he want?"

She shrugged. Even that hurt, but she wouldn't let him know. "If it was a *he*."

"I tend to think a man would rough-house you like that."

"I think I was responsible for hurting my face. I felt faint, and I had time to reason out that if I sank to the ground, they wouldn't dare drag me away from there unconscious. His or her intention was to get me into a Toyota parked at the end of the driveway. Someone could see us."

"That's something to go on. Whoever did this evidently owns a Toyota."

She nodded. "A lot of people in Webster City own Toyotas. The dealership is right up the street."

Once inside the suite, Laura went into the bathroom to clean her scraped face while Charles called Craig and informed him of the incident, repeating exactly what Laura had told him.

"Did she get hurt?"

"The scrapes and scratches are superficial. I'll get a better look when she's done cleaning it up, but I didn't see anything deep." He added softly, "She doesn't like what she sees in the mirror."

"You can't blame a woman for that. Shouldn't she go to the ER?"

"I don't think it's necessary, but if it gets any worse, I'll insist on it."

"Do you want me to come over to the hotel?"

"Laura said we have to meet Brad at the Pump House."

"He said he was going to try to catch Alvin Freeman today. He seemed pretty sure he could sneak up on him before he could run off. Are you sure Laura should go along?"

He sighed. "Neither you nor I have a choice. She's determined to find out who's threatening her and if someone actually did murder Scofield." A thought came to him that just in case Freeman was the one who did this to her, he was going to watch his reaction carefully when he first looked at Laura with her scrapes and scratches.

"Obviously, you know her better than I do."

"For whatever it's worth, I have six years of her life to catch up on. She's different, yet the same in so many ways. She has, however, grown into an independent woman who knows what she wants."

Craig chuckled. "I guess that happens to most women sooner or later. It's a good quality . . . most of the time. You'll get used to it. I'll catch up to you later."

They hung up as Laura walked into the room, holding a washcloth on her face. When Charles looked at her expecting tears, she said, "Don't say a word. Let's go."

On the way to meet Brad, Laura explained that the only way she thought of saving herself and foiling that person's plans was to pretend to faint. She said she sank to the ground and hit the side of her face on the sandy pavement. "Whoever had tried to abduct me didn't or couldn't hold on to me to prevent me from falling, and didn't bother to pick me up or drag me to the car. That made me think it could have been a woman."

"Or a man who wouldn't want to be seen dragging you against your will."

She sighed. "I'm so sorry I wasn't more careful. No, I'm sorry that I was trying to save time and run to the car while you were on the phone. I'll take this more seriously from now on."

"Maybe it's a lesson learned now that could save your life later. From now on, we stick together. Got it?"

She looked at him sheepishly. "Got it." She answered softly.

When they drove into the back lot of the Pump House, Brad was there waiting. He got out of his car and saw Laura's face. He rushed over to them. "What happened?"

Charles winked at Brad, hoping he wouldn't make too much of it. Laura's nerves were far from normal and she was too sensitive for her own good. "Someone tried to abduct her in the hotel parking lot."

"Who was it?"

She shrugged, and found that her arm really hurt when she did. "I couldn't tell."

"Man or woman?"

Charles cut in. "I saw a cap and a mustache, but that could have been a disguise."

Laura was surprised. "It could have been either a man trying to sound like a woman, or a woman lowering her voice to sound like a man."

Charles pointed to the back seat. "Ride with us. Alvin might recognize your car."

Brad crawled into the back seat. "Good idea." He winced when he saw Laura's face close up. "How on earth--"

"I don't want to talk about it." She was silent for a moment. "It isn't easy to admit that I shouldn't have tried to go out alone, but it was broad daylight."

"Our suspect isn't too sharp."

Charles mulled that over in his mind. "It may be that he or she is sharper than we think. That may have been done to throw us off."

Brad nodded. "Possible, but how would they know you'd go out the back door?"

"My car was parked in the back lot." Laura's voice was raspy and her words were short and clipped. She needed to direct Brad's attention away from herself. "Are you going to come up with more suspects?"

"Probably not." Brad told Charles the address and they discussed the possibility that they might catch him this time.

As they approached the place, Brad called Alvin's number. When someone answered, his eyes lit up and he nodded with success. "I'm callin' for an Alvin Freeman. Is that you, sir?" He spoke with an accent, but neither Charles nor Laura could tell if he was trying for a southern dialect or a Texas drawl. An actor he was not. He listened. "Ah'm callin' to ask a favor of ya. . . . . Ah know, ah know. Ah get that all the time. You're all too busy. It'll just take a minute of your time, sir." Charles stopped the car and Brad got out, still talking. Brad motioned that he would go to the front door, and that Charles should watch the side entrance. There evidently was no back door.

Charles nodded as he was on his way to the side door. He watched Brad ring the doorbell, but nobody answered. Just as Brad turned to come back, Laura spotted a man coming out of the side door. Before Charles could get to him, a tall man jumped into a dark green SUV and sped off down the alley.

Brad and Charles ran and climbed in the car. "Follow that car."

It was a serious moment, but Laura wanted badly to laugh. Her face, however, hurt too much. Hadn't she often seen movies with the exact circumstance? *Follow that car* was typical dialogue for crime movies and comedies.

Charles tried to pick up speed enough to catch up with the SUV, but one quick turn ahead had Charles pounding his fist on the steering wheel as he was stopped by the red light. "We lost him."

"It was definitely Alvin," said Laura. "And if you two didn't notice, he was driving a dark green SUV, just like Carol Harding's. Craig won't be so sure now that it was Carol who tried to run me down."

"It's going to make things sticky." Brad had another thought. "Okay, so here's the thing. Carol and Al have been getting cozy every once in a while for the last six years. Maybe they share the car. I'll have to check with DMV."

"Whoever was trying to get me today, wanted me to get into a Toyota."

"What color?"

She tried to think. "I was close to passing out, and the sun was glaring off the windshield, but I think it was tan or gold."

"That helps." Brad wrote it into his notebook.

Charles shook his head. "I'm sorry I let him get away, Brad."

"Hey, how many times do you think he's done this to *me*? He's one slippery character. I thought I had him pinned down, but he must have seen me out a window. I should have let you get to the side entrance first." He let out a sigh of disgust. "I didn't want to put you in danger by asking that of you." He hit his head with the heel of his hand. "We may have to leave this up to the chief."

"He'll have every right to question him since he drives a dark green SUV." Charles glanced over at Laura. She was very quiet. "What's the matter?" he asked.

"I don't know," she said thoughtfully. "Something is bothering me, but I don't know what it is."

Charles patted her hand. "It'll come."

Brad pulled out his cell phone. "I'll contact Chief Thomas. Maybe he'll want to meet us at the Pump House."

Twenty minutes later, they were in the back room with Craig waiting for them.

He immediately went to Laura and examined her bruises. His expression was serious, his eyes angry. "Tell me what happened to you. Don't leave anything out."

"Someone came up behind me and put his or her arm around my neck, choking me. I was supposed to get into a Toyota."

Craig moved behind her. "Like this?" He used his hand to choke her.

"No. The arm was here. He or she didn't have a hand on my neck at all." She moved his arm so that it was around her neck, with the crook of his elbow under her chin.

"All right. Like this?"

"Exactly."

"And you can't see if I'm a woman or a man."

She shook her head. "Something's not quite right, but I don't know what. Why can't I think of it?"

"You're still affected by the traumatic experience. Take it easy for a while," he said kindly. "If and when you think of what it is that bothers you, call me. I'm going back to the hotel and question some more people."

"More?"

Craig nodded, "I questioned anyone who might have seen in back of the building. The kitchen staff and laundry people saw only a man with a mustache, but they had no idea who he was or why he was there. They didn't get a good look at him."

"Or her. It could be a disguise."

Craig nodded and turned to Brad. "Tell me about Alvin Freeman."

"He got away again. I think you're going to have to use your authority so you can question him."

"On what grounds?"

All three answered. "He drives a dark green SUV."

Craig grunted. "That sort of muddies the waters, doesn't it?"

They nodded, all in agreement. Until today, Carol had been their prime suspect for wanting Laura out of the way. It was well known that she had an intense dislike for Laura, but he'd learned nothing more about the woman. She was short by any standards, probably no more than five feet one or two in shoes. Certainly her stature alone was enough to make her feel inferior to Laura who stood proudly at five-nine. Add that to her jealousy of Laura's ability and Scofield's romantic attention, Carol was his first choice of all the suspects, and they were getting far too many of them.

Craig questioned people in and around the hotel to see if they remembered seeing anyone in the rear parking lot or with a young woman. He'd given Laura's description. Nobody saw anything, but one woman said she'd seen a man who was rather short standing by the dumpster when she walked her dog down the alley. No, she hadn't noticed a Toyota there, but that didn't mean it wasn't there. She did notice that the man wore a cap so it was hard to see his face, but he had a mustache. From the first he had heard about it, Craig expected it to be a man simply because it's the sort of thing a man would do. Unless he missed his guess, only a man would disable a woman the way Laura had explained was done to her. He was, however, well aware of the self-defense classes that had sprung up for women. Still, he couldn't help thinking it was a man, but who?

His suspects were Alvin Freeman, Ed Langston or the latest one, Stuart Engleman, who proved to be a possible suspect in Scofield's death. The first two could resent Laura for her talent alone, but there was no evidence so far that the latter had anything against her. Which one had a mustache? Would he shave it off in case someone had seen him? Or was it a disguise?

The women suspects were Carol Harding and Cindy Meyer. They were suspects in Scofield's death as well as the threats Laura received. Neither had a mustache, of course, but they could have disguised themselves for fear of being seen. He sighed, wondering why these facts hadn't been revealed six years ago. The person driving the SUV that tried to run Laura down could be either man or woman, Carol, Ed or Cindy and possibly Al Freeman.

His day had started out just fine until he learned of Laura's attempted abduction. He didn't want to see anyone get hurt and most definitely not Laura. He should probably tell Brad and Laura to give up questioning people. Innocent people shouldn't get hurt. On the other hand, Brad was a reporter. They tended to take chances to get their story, but Laura and Charles shouldn't be involved. What was wrong with these people? Did it all have to do with Scofield? Is there more to it than meets the eye? Either way, he wanted to resolve this case so life could get back to normal for everyone.

He would have to call them in for questioning, at which time Laura could stand on the other side of the one-way mirror. She would be able to see and hear each suspect. One thing was sure. If Brad, Laura and Charles kept questioning people, he'd better do it soon before they came up with more suspects. He sighed heavily. Sometimes, it just didn't pay to get out of bed.

Brad left the Pump House first. He'd said goodbye to Laura and Charles before he left the back room. Things were not going smoothly. What made him think it was easy to solve a murder that happened six years ago. He had a few more former students to interview, and he would go ahead with the college staff who taught here then. He had already questioned the maintenance man and the school nurse. The secretary had been out of town, but would be back tomorrow. He knew nothing about the people at the bookstore. Some of them might have been here six years ago, but he was told that mostly students were employed as clerks. He'd leave that until last.

"Let's do something special today," said Charles as he headed for the room across the hall. They had done everything they could to help Craig and Brad. It was up to them now. In fact, they hadn't heard from either one for three days.

Laura had bought a large sheet of poster board and had written all the names and motives on it just as Craig had done on the blackboard. It was frustrating because it didn't get them anyplace. Laura was getting more depressed as each day passed.

"What did you have in mind?"

He shrugged. "What would be fun?"

"I'm not sure I know what *fun* is."

He frowned, concerned. "Didn't you ever do anything that made you happy?"

The look on her face was blank. "Six years ago, maybe. What *did* we do then?"

He tried to remember, but came up with nothing. He was beginning to see what she meant. They hadn't had time to do much except talk because their studies were so demanding. Charles had opted for a heavier load each semester to get done in three years. Laura had a normal load, but was taking voice, piano and organ lessons which each required an hour a day practice. That was on top of her regular classes that demanded preparation and study time. Drama meant practicing and memorizing lines that sometimes took hours. No wonder she was out of her element when he mentioned *fun*.

"Maybe we have to go back farther in time." She tried to think of high school, but that didn't apply. Her friends always wanted to go to where the boys hung out. Although she didn't want to, she went along just to belong to the group. They went to movies. That was it. "We could go to a movie. I haven't seen one in years. Have you?"

He shook his head. "I never learned French and I detest captions below the picture."

"Then how about it? Can we find a movie that would interest us?"

"I don't know why not? What's your pleasure, Laura?"

She got the entertainment section of the newspaper. As she opened it and laid it on the table, Charles was behind her and put his arm over her shoulder.

Laura looked up suddenly. "I remember," she said excitedly.

"Remember what?"

She stood up straight. "When that person tried to choke me." She pulled his arm over her shoulder just the way it was that day. "Your hand has to extend to my other shoulder so the crook of your elbow is here under my chin."

"Like this?" he asked, careful not to put any pressure on her throat."

"Yes, but . . . It's different. When you had your arm there before, there was weight on my shoulder. There isn't now."

"Of course not. Look, I'm taller than you. When we were looking at the paper, I was standing back a little. It would be the same if I were shorter. Look." He scrunched down a little and the weight was there, just as it had been that day.

Her face lit up. "That's it. Whoever it was must have been short."

"That narrows down the suspects."

"I'm going to call Craig."

An hour later, Craig parked his car in front of Carol Harding's apartment. He had called first to make sure she was home, but had not said he wanted to question her about any particular thing. He simply asked if she could give him some information about Laura. He hoped that he would ask the right questions so she wouldn't become suspicious of his motives. He wasn't sure how intelligent she was, or how shrewd. They were two different things, but either could spoil his interrogation.

Carol opened the door and invited Craig into her apartment. It was neat and furnished with comfortable furniture. What he assumed were family pictures were on one wall and others on end tables.

"I hate to take your time like this, but I need to know if you know anything about Stuart Engleman's relationship to Laura Westlund." He knew that involving Laura would get to Carol.

Carol frowned. "I don't think I know him. Did he say he knew me?"

"No. I just thought that you were students at the same time. Do you know of anyone who drives a late model tan or gold Toyota?"

"I've seen many of them, but do I know anyone who has one?" She took time to think back. "No. I'm afraid I don't. What is this about?"

"Just a complaint that was filed. While I'm here, maybe you'll clear up some other things."

"Like what?"

"You told me that Scofield confided in you about many things." He watched her eyes as she sat up a little straighter. He would try to determine how far she'd go to get Laura into trouble and make herself seem uninvolved. "You said that Laura was responsible for Scofield's death six year ago. How can you be sure of that? When was the last time you saw him alive?"

"Well," she said stalling, "I'll have to think about that. After all, six years is a long time to remember something that means nothing to me." Craig's look of surprise told her that she'd made a mistake. "That is, something that really didn't concern me."

"Do you mean to say that his death didn't concern you?"

"N-no. I'm saying at the time, it meant nothing to me because I knew where I stood with Freddie. He wanted me, but he was caught up in this prestige thing."

"You'll have to explain that to me. I'm not into the politics of culture and music."

"Well, Laura had already been chosen for the concert tour. I told you about that before. Freddie said that I should have had the tour, but that he had to nominate Laura because of, as you put it, college politics. It was prestige for the college to have the student who received the student-of-the-year award, be awarded the concert tour. Naturally, she was ecstatic about it and she let everybody know. She was a prima donna from way back. She still is, if you haven't talked to her lately."

Craig was going to lose his patience very soon, and that would not be good. "I just don't know about such things." *If she didn't see Laura going to the police station, could she have been the one who tried to run her down? Maybe she was trying to throw him off.* "I'll have to take your word for it, but that still doesn't answer my question."

Looking very innocent, Carol asked, "Which question was that?"

She was a cagey one. "When you last saw Scofield."

"Let me think. He was found a few days after graduation, wasn't it?"

She'd known exactly when it was the last he'd questioned her. "It was right after graduation. The coroner said his death was sometime between ten-thirty and one o'clock in the morning."

She nodded slowly, thinking back. "I guess I saw him after the graduation exercises, around ten o'clock maybe. I can't be too sure exactly." Then she opened her eyes wide, obviously in actress mode again. "I must have been the last person to see him before he took all those pills."

"Had he been drinking at all?"

"Why, yes. I remember thinking it strange because he acted almost like he was drunk. I'd never seen him that drunk before."

"So he drank as a habit?"

She shrugged. "Doesn't everyone?"

"Some do, some don't. It's a matter of personal conviction. I understand that you spoke to Laura Westlund when she was here for the concert."

She wondered how he could have learned about that. "Yes, I did. Is there a reason you're asking?"

"Just that the hotel desk clerk said he had to intervene. He said you were quite belligerent."

"With good reason," she snapped. "Look, are you trying to tell me I shouldn't have told her what I thought of her?"

He shook his head with his best innocent expression. "I'm just repeating what the clerk said. Don't let it bother you. Just to clear things up, the desk clerk said it sounded like you were jealous of Laura."

Carol's face turned beet red with anger. "Why would I be jealous of her? I told you, all I cared about was what Freddie thought of me and my talent. The rest didn't matter."

"I see." He stood up. "I may have to ask you to come into the station to answer these questions formally and sign a statement. I hope you don't mind the imposition."

Her eyes darted back and forth. Finally she sighed. "If it will help any, just let me know when." She smiled, but the smile didn't reach her eyes.

He'd give anything to know what she was thinking. He couldn't wait to get her into the interrogation room at the station. The room intimidated people who'd been cool and calm in previous questionings, supposedly just to get information in a friendly way. Most felt like they were doing the chief a favor. That's what he wanted them to think. If they felt threatened, they'd have no intention of being helpful.

As Craig got into his car, he wondered if Carol would be able to remember which lies she told. That tripped the best of them up. It was one reason he'd wanted to question her again before he brought her in for the formal interrogation. He took out his notebook and jotted down a few facts before starting the car.

First thing tomorrow, he'd set up the interrogations so Laura, Brad and Charles could listen and compare what they said with what they were told before. It should prove to be interesting.

Chapter 10

It was a gloomy and rainy Monday morning. Laura and Charles had breakfast in the coffee shop. They looked out the window at the dismal sky. It was the kind of day that you'd like to stay inside and curl up with a good book. Inside, however, it was bright and cheery and the bubbly waitress quoted the menu with enthusiasm. Cheerful conversations were taking place all around them. It was almost as if they had waited months for a drought to end.

Most of the guests were older and appeared to be very much at home here. Some looked at each other with admiration, love or humor, but never anger. They looked like they had all the time in the world and they probably did. Laura wondered if she and Charles would ever get to that place in time when they would be settled into their relationship, happy to be with each other. All her life, when she thought about getting older, it was troubling, almost scary. She wasn't sure what made her dread aging. Maybe it was that she'd had nobody to love when Charles left for Paris. But being with him today was such a pleasant thought that Laura was actually looking forward to growing old with Charles. She wondered if he felt the same way.

After the waitress took their orders, Charles approached the subject of their scheduled meeting at the police station. He didn't dare say too much for fear of being overheard, but he wasn't quite convinced that Laura should stand face to face with the suspects Craig intended to interrogate. "But for these people to see you and know why you're there," he shook his head, "I think it's too risky."

"Oh, Charles, I'm sorry," she whispered. "We'll be in another room. We'll be able to see them and hear them, but they won't know we're there. It's like you see in the movies when someone has to identify a particular person and pick him out of a line up."

Charles chuckled. "Of course. I should have known better. I just don't want anything to happen to you, and if you were to be responsible for identifying one of them," he shrugged, "you know that person wouldn't take it kindly. I, for one, am personally going to see to it that you won't be in danger."

Laura laughed. "I already am, and I'm sure because you're with me, that puts you in danger, too."

"I can handle that. I *couldn't* handle it if anything happened to you."

Her eyes looked at him with so much love, he wanted to scoop her up and take her out of here to someplace he could speak freely instead of whispering so others couldn't hear. "We'll be fine. It sounds like we're finally getting down to business. I can only hope that it won't be long now."

"Then what?"

She wanted him to say what would happen next. She had always been shy and it would be too hard for her to say what she was hoping for. Even if she was sure Charles knew, it was important to her that it come from his mouth, not hers. "What would you like to do when this is all over?"

He closed his eyes briefly, trying to keep his manner calm, without advertising to the other guests what was on his mind.

"We meet again." The words came from a man who had approached their table.

"Ed Langston," said Laura. "How are you?" What else could she say?

"Still in town?" His expression was angry. "Don't you have business elsewhere?"

Charles stood up. "Does it matter to you where she is or what she's doing here?"

Ed looked around the room. "You're darn right it does. She has no business here. Why don't you go home, or take a flying leap to the moon for all I care. Just leave. You're not wanted here." Before either one could answer, he turned on his heel and left.

Charles and Laura looked at each other as the waitress brought their food. "I see old Ed is up to no good again," she said. "The manager told him to leave the other day. I didn't think he'd come back. What is it with him? Everyplace he goes, he threatens someone or causes trouble one way another." She shook her head. "I apologize."

"It's certainly not your fault," said Charles.

"I'll tell the manager as soon as he comes back." She looked up to see him walking in the door. "He's here now. Ed must have seen him coming and made a quick exit. You're lucky. You should have heard him the other night. He picked a fight with someone named Alvin. They were ready to fight it out with their fists." She asked if they wanted more coffee before she left their table.

"Alvin?" said Laura, looking at Charles. Was he thinking what she was thinking?

After speaking to the waitress, the manager came to their table. "I understand Langston bothered you. I apologize. I don't know what's wrong with the man, but I'm thinking of taking out a restraining order on him. I don't want him bothering our guests."

"Thank you for caring," said Laura, "but it isn't your fault."

"Don't hesitate to let me know if something doesn't meet with your approval."

"Thank you." She waited until he left the table. "That was nice of him."

"It's nice to know people care."

Charles left a large tip for the waitress. He helped Laura into her jacket and they left the coffee shop.

When they approached the elevator, they could hear angry voices coming from the desk. Since one voice belonged to a woman, Charles went to see what was going on.

"You mind your own business, little lady and we'll do just fine. Now, answer me. Which room is Laura Westlund in?"

"I told you, sir. I can't give out that information."

Ed moved closer to her. "Look. She's a very good friend of mine and she won't like it one bit if you don't tell me where she is."

Laura walked right over to him. "I'm right here, Ed. I'm sorry; I didn't realize we were such good friends." Her words dripped with sarcasm.

Ed stood motionless, mouth open ready to speak, but nothing came out. His eyes threw darts at her as he mumbled some expletives. He turned and left.

"I do *not* like that man," said the desk clerk.

"I'm sure there aren't many who do," said Charles as they went to the elevator.

"What do you suppose he wanted?"

"I don't think it was anything good. However, one thought occurred to me. He didn't deliver the threats if he didn't know which room you were in."

"I'm trying to think back if I ever did anything to earn his dislike."

Charles chuckled. "Dislike? I'd be more inclined to say it 's more like loathing."

Charles went across the hall to check his messages, before he joined Laura in her suite. He sat down beside Laura on the sofa. "This is getting more confusing as time goes by. Unfortunately, I sense more danger, as well."

Laura agreed. "Charles," she said as she looked out the window as if to find answers out there, "I wonder if it wouldn't be safer for you if you went back to Chicago and waited for me there."

It was such a ridiculous thought that Charles would have laughed if it weren't so serious. He reached over and tapped her on the shoulder. "I was not referring to my safety, Laura. I was talking about *yours*. Do you honestly believe that I would for one minute leave you here to face this by yourself?"

"It would make me feel better. Just because someone is threatening me doesn't mean that you have to be threatened, too."

"Wild horses couldn't drag me away from you. Not ever again. Got it?"

She smiled weakly. "Got it, but--"

"No buts, sweetheart. I love you. I will not leave you. Please understand that I can't leave."

She sighed and nodded, feeling very much loved, but sad at the same time. She prayed that they would stay safe in God's hands. Surely He wouldn't allow evil to win over something like this."

Charles was watching her. "What's going on in that pretty little head of yours?"

She sighed again. "An age old question that keeps entering my mind."

"Which is?"

"Will God allow good to prevail or is there a reason He would allow evil to win?"

"Good one. And you're reasoning that evil often does win over good?"

"I don't know. I hope that somehow, the outcome is for good."

He nodded slowly. "Explain that to me."

She shrugged. "I read a story about a woman who had been so abused by her husband that she barely escaped with her life. When she tried to stand up to her husband, he vowed he would kill her and if she said anything to anyone, he would take their children away from her and keep her a prisoner until she would starve to death. The doctor who examined her after her husband *said* she was in a car accident could tell that she had been *beaten* to near death. He offered to help her escape and he did. The doctor was found dead in a car accident. On the surface, the good doctor died trying to save her and her children. She later got a letter that was left for her. She learned that he had a fast growing cancer and that he would have died in a matter of four or five months and that the last few months would have been very painful." She took a deep breath. "It's not the same thing, I know, but good did win and the doctor was saved a very painful few months. The woman and her children fled and went to a different country with a new identity." She smiled as she watched him. "I think it was based on a real life story."

He shook his head. "Beautiful story, but in this case, if evil wins, good loses."

"How can Ed's evil win and still make the outcome be for good?"

"It's possible, I'm sure. That doesn't mean that good people don't get hurt."

He sat up straight. This was getting him nowhere. There is no explanation for situations like this that any human can analyze. Laura needed cheering up, and this was certainly not doing her any good. "Will you play for me?"

She was glad that he'd changed the subject. "What would you like to hear?"

"Improvise. Show me through your music what you're feeling."

She smiled. How *was* she feeling? She certainly had mixed emotions. All the mess with Fredrick and the threats was only a part of it. As she looked at Charles, she was feeling loved and protected. She hoped that when she sat down at the piano that that feeling of love would stand out above all the turmoil and fear.

And it did. She played with her heart and Charles sat mesmerized by her beauty, her ability to let the music take him to a place only his imagination could take him. He wondered if she was feeling what he was feeling right now.

Brad sat with Craig in his office discussing Alvin Freeman's avoiding Brad. Craig had arranged for Carol to come to the office this afternoon to answer questions in front of a stenographer. When she was done, the testimony would be typed for Carol to sign.

"Carol Harding will be first because she's the most likely suspect."

Brad shook his head. "I think Al is equally suspicious. Why else would he avoid me? You didn't get to question him, either."

"True, but I'll get him into the station if I have to arrest him. If he resists arrest, that in itself is a crime and I can hold him for it."

Bard sighed. "Maybe you're right. I only hope he doesn't skip town if he finds out Carol is making a statement here."

Craig smiled. "I hope he finds out. He'll worry himself sick that she's spilling the beans. They can't have stayed together all this time and not be in cahoots."

"I agree, but he could skip out."

Craig smiled and tapped his head. "You think I don't know that? I have a man watching him until we bring him in. I want him to come in just as Carol is leaving. If that doesn't make him talk, nothing will."

Brad clapped a congratulatory hand on Craig's back. "Pretty sharp, Chief Thomas. I know why you got elected. Remind me to vote for you at the next election."

Craig shook his head. "This is my last year. I'm retiring."

"Because you want to or because--"

"Because my wife is retiring next year. We're going to see the world together."

Brad stood up and shook Craig's hand. "The best of luck to you. The people of Webster City are going to miss you."

He nodded a thank you to Brad for the compliment. "Be here at two o'clock and you can watch from the next room with Laura and Templeton."

"I'll be here by one-thirty."

"Good. I'll see you then."

Brad left and Craig called Laura with his plans. It was all set. All three of them would be at the station and sit in the next room to watch and listen to Carol's testimony.

Craig paced the floor. He'd written the questions he was going to ask each of the suspects. With any luck, the timing would be just right so Al Freeman would see Carol leaving. If Carol saw him, too, that was even better. If they were both involved in any of this, each one would wonder what the other one said. That should be a definite advantage.

At one-thirty on the dot, Laura and Charles came into the station with Brad only minutes behind them. He'd seen them get out of their car, so he thought it best to wait until they were well inside before entering. Brad chuckled to himself. Laura might have the right idea about this being cloak and dagger stuff, but it wasn't a laughing matter, not with those threats. It was serious, and he hoped they would all remember it.

Craig showed them into the room next to the interrogation room. "You'll sit here." He pointed to the chairs. "There's coffee over there and some rolls in that bakery box. Help yourselves. It could be a long afternoon. I asked Carol Harding to come in at two. She thinks she's coming in to be formally interrogated in front of a stenographer so she can sign her statement. Once we're done with the questioning, the stenographer leaves the room to type up the statement. I've asked that she watch the time carefully, so she comes in shortly before Al Freeman is due in. I want them to see each other."

Laura frowned. "Why?"

"Because if you're partly right, they may both be involved. What's more, they might even be working together. If not, they will at least wonder what the other one has been telling me. My guess is that there will be two worried people by the time they leave the station this afternoon."

Charles shook his head. "That's what I said. Cloak and dagger stuff all the way. Even the CIA couldn't do better." He held out his hand to Craig. "I'm impressed."

Laura smiled. "I told you he was a special man."

Craig blushed and looked at his watch to avoid looking at them. "I'd better get into my office before Carol gets here."

Brad nodded with admiration. "Good luck with the questions."

Twenty minutes later, Craig showed Carol into the room and asked her to sit down in the chair. She looked around the room and was tempted to take the chair on the other side of the table, but the stenographer came in and sat down by the table where two chairs had been placed. Carol gave in and did as she was told. Why was she nervous? He said he was just going to question her again so she could sign a statement. She never gave him cause to think she had committed a crime.

"Well then," Craig looked at the stenographer. "Are you ready?"

She nodded.

Craig asked Carol to state her name, address and phone number, her birth date and her occupation. He asked about her affiliation with the college, when she attended, what she majored in, and other relevant questions. He was wasting time and getting her comfortable with talking, asking nothing incriminating.

Meanwhile, Laura, Charles and Brad sipped coffee, anxiously waiting for Craig to ask more important questions. They didn't speak to each other fearing that Carol would hear them. That was a question they forgot to ask.

"Were you acquainted with Professor Scofield?"

Carol looked angry. "I told you I was," she snapped.

Craig gave her a small smile. "We need this for the statement. You can forget what you told me before and just consider this the first time I'm asking. It will be easier on you and on your temper."

Carol squirmed in her chair and nodded.

"Were you acquainted with Professor Scofield?"

"Yes. I was his student."

"And what was the relationship between you and the professor?"

She took a deep breath trying to tamp down her temper. "He said I was a very good student, in fact, the best one he ever had."

Sure you were. "And was he able to show this fact in any way?"

"He said I should have had the student of the year award, but he had to nominate Laura Westlund because of," she shrugged, "college politics. Because of that award, I'm sure she got the tour contract. Freddie said I should have had that, too."

"Did you ever go out with the professor during the time you were a student?"

Carol stiffened up. "You didn't ask me that before."

"I didn't think of it then. Sorry, but please answer the question."

"He took me to dinner once at the Copper Kettle, but I had to drive there myself and pretend that we just happened to see each other there. Nothing planned, you know."

"Why was that?"

"Well, students don't date teachers. The college frowns on that."

"Didn't you tell me that you saw him with Laura at a restaurant and at the opera?"

"Well, ah- yes."

"Doesn't that contradict what you just told me?"

"Well, ah- no. I'm pretty sure it was because she was chosen for the concert tour and he was just giving her a broad education so she would be more . . . well, you know, so she wouldn't behave like a country bumpkin and embarrass the college."

"I see." He hesitated for a minute. That question easily led to the next one which he hadn't quite known how do bring up. "Did you ever see them drinking together?"

"You mean drink alcohol?" she asked a little surprised. Her eyes went from one side to the other as if she were thinking. This might be her chance to blame a lot of things on Laura. "Well, I hate to get Laura into trouble, but yes. I saw them having wine during the intermission at the opera, and then at a restaurant, they ordered cocktails."

"Did you ever have drinks with him?"

"No. That is, not in public, but we drank wine at his place once in a while."

"Do you know of any reason that Scofield would have committed suicide?"

Her body jerked anxiously. "Why are you asking that?"

"Because he killed himself. Do you know what would cause him to do that?"

She shrugged. "You'd better ask Laura."

"All right." He took a deep breath. "I need to ask you if you were out of town at any of these times. He checked his watch and decided he'd better hurry now. "I'll write the dates down," he said as he wrote, "and you tell me if you were out of town. These are the days and dates." He shoved the paper over to her. "Take your time, because they won't be easy to remember."

Craig sat back to give her time and to study her expression. At first she seemed puzzled, but she quickly recovered and answered. "I was in Milwaukee from May tenth to the thirteenth. Outside of that, I was here. What is this all about?"

"Nothing to worry about." He nodded at the stenographer and she left the room. "So you do commercials for car dealers?" he asked to waste time.

"Not only for car dealers. There's a company in Webster City that does commercials for the entire the United States. I went into drama during my last two years at college. It paid off a lot better than my music, thanks to Laura. If I'd gotten that tour contract . . . oh well. It didn't happen." Her face was twisted with anger and jealousy.

Craig kept up the small talk until the stenographer returned with the papers to sign. "Look over the answers and sign it at the bottom of the last page when you're certain that they're correct and you'll be all done."

She signed the paper and stood up to leave.

"Thank you for coming in for this." He motioned her toward the door as he opened it and walked her through the central office to the door. Alvin was sitting on the bench, waiting to be called in. When he saw Carol, his eyes opened wide. Carol's eyes showed panic briefly. She got hold of herself and walked up to him. "Well, Alvin. Fancy meeting you here," she gushed. "Haven't seen you for ages. How've you been?"

Craig noticed the tone of Carol's voice, as if she were trying to warn Alvin of something. "I take it you two know each other."

Carol jumped in before Alvin could answer. "We went to college together, even had the same classes."

Alvin, confused because they'd just had dinner last week, wondered what she was up to. He nodded and watched Carol carefully. She sure did look strange and she sounded different, too. Was she trying to tell him something? Women! They had their own method of communication and men were supposed to be mind readers.

Craig showed Carol to the door and gestured for Alvin to follow him into the interrogation room. "Sit in that chair and I'll be back shortly." He closed the door and stepped into the next room. "Hear anything interesting?" he asked.

Laura whispered. "We didn't think we should talk in here."

Craig nodded. "You can talk softly, and we won't hear. If you talk loud, you'll give yourselves away."

Charles spoke, but kept his voice low. "So Scofield drank after all."

Craig shook his head. "No. I think Carol is covering her rear. I'd bet my pension that she's trying to throw all suspicion from herself onto you, Laura."

"I'll buy that." Brad moved forward to look through the glass at Al."

"I'd better get in there." Craig left them and joined Alvin and the stenographer.

"I've tried to call you a few times. I'm glad we managed to pin you down."

Alvin was irritated and didn't mind showing it. "What is this all about?"

"Routine questions." He started with the name, address, occupation and the information he already had in Al's file. Routine questions calmed him down. After a few more question, Craig jumped right into the heavy questions. "How well did you know Professor Scofield?"

He shrugged. "As well as any of his students. What is this about?"

"Just answer the questions. The stenographer is taking down your answers and I'll ask you to check it over and sign it when she gets it typed up."

"You mean like a confession?"

Craig had a smile on his lips. "I don't know. Do you have something to confess?"

That made Al uncomfortable. "What do you want to know?"

"Your friend, Carol, had quite a bit to say about Laura Westlund. What can you tell me about her?"

He shrugged. "What do you want to know?"

"Anything you can tell me. Was she well liked when she was attending college?"

"For the most part, but not by everyone."

"Explain that."

"Well, some of the students felt she was given privileges. Scofield practically adopted her."

"Which students didn't like it?"

Al hesitated. If he lied now and had to take a lie detector test later, they'd have him. "There was a Barbara Henley, ah – Ed Langston and a guy named ah-" he grated his teeth while he thought, finally snapping his fingers. "Stu Engleman."

"What about Carol Harding?"

Tough one, he thought. What had she told them? Better tell him. "Yeah. She said Scofield had to give the award to Laura because of politics." He shrugged his shoulders. "I never did find out what she meant by that. She should have had the award, you know."

"Was she that good?"

Al sighed. "I don't really know. She thought she was and she said Scofield told her she was."

Craig narrowed his eyes. "Did you believe her?"

"Why not?"

"I don't know. You tell me."

"She might have exaggerated, I suppose. Laura's good. Damn good, if you ask me. I went to her concert, you know. She really knows how to put on a good show. People eat that up."

"You think she's insincere?"

"What do I know? Why all the questions?"

"We're not nearly done, so be patient." Craig looked at his notes. "Between May ninth and May twentieth, were you out of town?"

"I've been out of town a lot. I went to Rockford the first part of May and

I spent three days in Chicago."

"When was that?"

"Hmmm. May thirteenth to the fifteenth."

"Did you see Laura then?"

"No. Why should I?"

"She had her concert in Chicago on May fifteenth."

"I didn't know that. Besides I got back to town at about three in the afternoon."

"Can you think of anything to tell me about Professor Scofield? According to the people here, he was well liked."

"For the most part. I suppose by people who didn't have him for a teacher."

"But what about the people who *did* know him?"

"Well, there was the teacher's pet thing, but he was a good teacher, a little high handed maybe."

"How so?"

"He kicked Ed Langston out of his class and sent him to another teacher."

"I've heard that. Do you know why?"

Al wasn't about to squeal, but he'd better tell the truth. He didn't like any of this. He shouldn't have stuck that note under Laura's door just because he was afraid of what would happen if Carol saw Laura. So what? It was none of his business, and Carol could be pretty bitchy when she didn't get her way.

"You're stalling, Al. What do you have on your mind?"

"Scofield found out that Ed Langston was using drugs."

Craig nodded. "Have you ever used?"

"Me? Not really," he said slowly.

"Not really? What does that mean?"

He fidgeted before answering. "I guess I have a couple of times before I wised up. It's not a good thing."

"Can you tell me where you were on May tenth?"

He shrugged. "What happened May tenth?"

"Just answer the question, Al."

"I was at the clinic that day. I had a little surgery, and they made me stay until the anesthetic wore off."

"Which clinic?"

He was becoming prickly. "Why are you asking that?"

"Answer the question."

"Webster Medical Clinic."

"One last thing. Did you leave a note for Laura while she was in Webster City?"

How the heck did he find out? Damn. Did he have any choice? He sighed deeply. "Okay, so I left her a note. So what?"

"What did the notes say?"

"Whoa. Not notes. One. Singular."

"Only one?"

"Only one," he repeated decisively.

"What did it say?"

He shrugged. "Something like Go home."

"Did you write it in pen and ink?"

"Are you kidding? No way. I cut the words out of magazines."

"What day was that?"

"It was a Sunday, the day after her concert."

"Why did you want her out of town?"

"Because Carol was making noises about telling her off. When she loses her temper, you don't want to be around her. Believe me, I know."

"So you were protecting Laura?"

"Hell, no. I was protecting myself. Whenever Carol got mad, she took it out on me. She'd rant and rave and make my life a living hell."

"Why did you let her?"

He shrugged. "I keep thinking she'll settle down some day so we can, you know, get together."

Craig nodded. "Well," he sighed, "I think that's about all for now." He told the stenographer to type up the paper and bring them back for his signature."

Al was uncomfortable. "Can I ask you a question?"

"You can ask."

"Why did you ask about May tenth?"

Craig reasoned that maybe if he told him the truth, he might get more information from him. "You own a dark green SUV?"

Al nodded. "So?"

"A dark green SUV tried to run Laura down on that day."

Al's face turned pale. "You're kidding, aren't you?"

Craig shook his head. "You wouldn't happen to know who else has a green SUV, would you?"

"Sure. You'd find out, anyway. Carol has one."

"Would she do anything that drastic?"

Al was silent. "I don't know. I hope not, but I really don't know. Hell, if she did it, I don't want anything to do with her. She's dangerous."

"Are you sure you didn't deliver more than the one note?"

"Absolutely. Why would I?"

The stenographer came back, handed the pages to Al to look over before signing his name. Craig then thanked him and showed him out.

He went back to the room where Laura, Brad and Charles were waiting; "Well, what do you think?"

Brad answered. "I think we're getting more than we bargained for. Al delivered the first note. That leaves all the others. Carol could have done the others."

"Except for the one in Chicago. She has an air tight alibi for the whole day."

"Craig," said Laura, "why didn't you ask them where they were on the specific dates I got the notes."

"We know when you noticed them, but we don't know what time and for a couple, what day they were delivered. They could easily wiggle out of that."

"What now?" asked Charles.

"I called Cindy Meyer and Stuart Engleman to come into the station tomorrow. Cindy will be here at ten and Stuart at eleven I have to tell you, I think questioning Engleman is a waste of time, but I'll check him out. Maybe he can throw some light on the whole thing. He may not be guilty of anything, but he might know something about someone who is."

Charles frowned. "What about Ed Langston?"

"He'll be out of town all day tomorrow. He might find time to come in the next day. He'll call me."

"Can we come back tomorrow and listen?"

"By all means."

Brad walked out of the station a few minutes before the others. Laura and Charles stayed to go over what they had learned. In case anyone was watching, they would have no reason to connect Brad to Laura and Charles. Let them think that everyone is being questioned, everyone except Brad, that is. Lately, he often came into the station looking for a story. Nobody would think anything of it.

Craig looked at Laura. "I'm assuming that Al will talk to Carol and let her know that you've had several notes. If I read him right, he's no longer enchanted with her. In fact, I'm sure he wonders just how far Carol would go to take her hatred out on you. You have to be careful. Unless I miss my guess, she's like a bomb ready to explode.

Laura nodded. This whole thing still didn't seem real, but she knew it was dangerous to think that way.

"We'll be careful." said Charles, leading her out. "See you tomorrow?"

"You bet," Charles shook his hand.

"I'm glad she has you to watch over her."

Laura nodded. "So am I."

Chapter 11

Laura and Charles were seated in the room next to the interrogation room, drinking coffee. Laura was thinking over what Carol had said and how Alvin seemed to be disgusted with her actions, or the actions he thought she might be responsible for. "Do you think Carol wrote those notes?"

Charles was thoughtful. "I don't know. The fact that Alvin wrote the first one clarifies the difference in the notes and the messages."

"The first one isn't nearly as threatening as the others," said Laura. "Whoever wrote them seems to be gathering more and more steam."

"Steam? Evil describes those notes better."

"Remember that Craig said Carol had an alibi for the one you got in Chicago."

Laura nodded. "But she could have had someone else deliver it, couldn't she?"

"And that person could have been Alvin."

"Possibly, but could he be that good an actor? He sounded genuinely surprised and upset at the thought that Carol might have tried to run me down. His body language told more than his words."

Brad entered the room. "Good morning."

Charles nodded a greeting as Brad poured himself some coffee. "What do think about yesterday?"

Brad drank half his coffee down in one gulp, showing obvious pleasure.

"Late night?" asked Laura, amused.

"Research kept me busy, but I need my morning coffee."

"What did you think about yesterday? You left before I could ask."

"I don't know what to think right now. The information I came up with last night didn't help one bit." He looked at his watch. "Who's first this morning?"

"Cynthia Meyer."

Just then, they saw Craig enter with the stenographer and Cindy. He told her to sit at the other side of the table.

"What is this all about?" She was indignant, to say the least.

Craig kept his voice calm. "Just some routine questions for now."

"What do you mean *for now?*" she snapped.

Craig wanted to jump right into the questions, but he knew by taking his time, Cindy would be less agitated and was likely to say more than she intended. He slowly looked over his notes. After listening to her sighs, he finally started. "State you name, address, phone number and age."

In the next room, Laura leaned close to Charles. "Why is he taking so long?"

"He's trying to make her relax. Didn't you see how fidgety she was?"

Brad nodded. "He's giving her time to hang herself." He grinned.

Laura couldn't help thinking it wasn't fair if Cindy wasn't part of this. Still, she'd never been likable and had done her best to belittle Laura. Also, she'd stolen her musical.

Craig went on. "Have you been out of town during May?"

Her head snapped up. "Why do you want to know?"

"Miss Meyer, we are not going to get anyplace if you keep avoiding answers by asking questions of your own. I understood you to say you'd be glad to cooperate."

She calmed herself. "I am. I just don't know what you want to know?"

"Let me put it this way? If you're going to answer me truthfully, does is matter why I'm asking you? Would you answer any differently if you knew why I'm asking?"

She knew how that would affect her whole testimony. She felt foolish and didn't want the chief to know. "No, of course not."

"Then answer the question. Have you been out of town during May?"

She thought about it. "I was in Madison, Wisconsin on May eighth and in Milwaukee on the . . . it was a Friday." She glanced at the calendar on the wall. "The fourteenth."

"That's it?"

"That's it."

How well did you know Professor Scofield?

"Why would you want to know that? He's been dead for six years."

"Yes. I'm well aware of that. Just answer the question."

She sighed heavily. "We taught together at the college."

"Were you friends, acquaintances, enemies?"

She huffed. "We certainly weren't enemies." Her eyes went around the room as if stalling for time to think. "I had the feeling that Fred was interested in a relationship."

"And you weren't?"

"Why do you need to know that? Is nothing private?" Craig sighed, so she went on. "I don't know if I was or not. He was nice, but there was just something about him that wasn't quite right."

"And what was that?"

She shook her head. "I don't know. I can't put it into words. He was just so changeable. One day he was interested in what I said; the next, he didn't know I existed."

"I understood that when he was hired, they gave him your title of Department Head. Did that bother you?"

"Yes. A lot, but I understood that the college wasn't doing well financially, and when they were able to get such a famous name, they had to give him the title. It didn't hurt any less, but I understood."

"And when he died? Did you get your title back?"

She looked over her glasses. "You must be aware that I didn't. They gave it to Melissa McAllister."

"And how did you feel about that?"

Irritated at the question, her mouth formed a thin straight line. "How would you feel if they made you a Deputy?"

Craig nodded. "All right. How well do you know Laura Westlund?"

"As well as anyone." Her eyes were filled with suspicion. "Why are you asking?"

Craig just looked at her this time. He wanted her to worry a little. Sooner or later, she would say something to break the uncomfortable silence.

"Laura was Fred's student, not mine."

"I understand that the college gave a performance recently."

Her body stiffened. "If you're talking about the musical, yes. We performed one this month. What are you getting at?" Her face turned red with anger.

"The program stated that you wrote it. Did you?"

"Part of it."

"Part of it? Who wrote the other part?"

Cindy put her head down. "Laura Westlund," she said quietly, but suddenly her voice became loud and her chin rose defensively. "She wrote it as a student. Manuscripts that are written by students for class become the property of the college."

"Is that legal?"

"Why not?" She watched Craig study her face. "Isn't it?"

"You tell me."

She became more defensive. "There was no name on the manuscript and it was in Professor Scofield's file. He intended to perform it. Why shouldn't we?"

"You know the answer to that. Did you contact Miss Westlund about using it?"

"I told you that there was no name on it."

"You can't tell me that you didn't know she wrote it."

She could tell by his expression that he knew. What could she say? She sighed deeply. "Okay. I knew, but I needed something to show the college I was capable. Fred got my title; then, Melissa. I had nothing but teaching behind me. I needed some kind of accomplishment. What can they do to me?" she asked in a small voice.

"That depends on Miss Westlund and the college. Did they ever tell you why they didn't give you your title back?"

Cindy stared at him blankly. She lowered her head and mumbled. "They said I was too antagonistic about it and I talked to too many people."

"That would do it in my book," he said in defense of the college.

She wished she could walk out, but she didn't dare. "Is there anything else?"

"Did you know that Miss Westlund's life was threatened?"

"No. When did that happen?"

"It doesn't matter. Is there anything else you can tell me about Scofield or his students? He had a couple really promising ones."

"Yes. I understood Ed Langston was brilliant for a while. I don't know what happened. He slipped to mediocre or less."

"How did he feel about Miss Westlund?"

"How would I know?"

He nodded and stood up, signaled the stenographer to type up the notes. "It won't take her long to type up the papers and bring them in for your signature. Would you like coffee while you wait?"

She shook her head. She just wanted to be left alone. When he left the room, her head sank into her hands. *What have I done?*

When Cindy had signed the papers and left, Craig was about to go into the next room when he was informed that Stuart Engleman had arrived.

Stuart had answered the preliminary questions. Craig asked about the dates he was out of town. He hadn't been. When he was asked about his relationship to Laura, he hesitated.

"I hardly knew her. Well, I knew *of* her, but our paths didn't cross, no classes together or anything like that." He took a deep breath. "Don't get me wrong. I would like to have known her, but she was way out of my league and I knew it."

"How about Professor Scofield?"

"Now that's a different matter. I couldn't stand his guts."

"Why was that?"

"He accused me of cheating and I hadn't been. I asked to get out of his class but he wouldn't allow it until the end of the semester. I had to see him week after week for my lessons. He didn't budge either." He looked a little sheepish. "I didn't either. I refused to practice. He gave me the grades I deserved." He shook his head. "I didn't hurt anyone but myself, but," he shrugged, "I was young. But it still infuriates me that he thought I was cheating. I never have and I never would cheat for any reason."

"How did other students feel about him?"

"Some hated him, some thought he was great."

"How about the faculty?"

"I saw Miss Meyer leave. She was one unhappy lady and everybody knew it. Then, there was some kind of argument between another professor and him."

"Who?"

"I'm not sure what it was about, but Professor Standish was furious with him for some reason."

Craig nodded and asked him about a few more insignificant things before one last question. "Do you know of anyone who would want to hurt Laura Westlund?"

"Hurt her? No way. She was just a great girl, a wonderful pianist. You probably heard that she gave a concert here a while back."

"I heard. Well, if you can't think of anything else I should know, I'll have the papers typed up for you to sign."

A few minutes later, Craig entered the next room. "Can you take one more suspect?"

Brad smiled. "Ed Langston?"

Craig nodded. "I saved the best for last."

Laura and Charles both frowned. "Why is he the best?"

"It wasn't until I spoke with him on the phone, but you'll figure it out. He's due here in about five minutes. I'll go out front and wait for him. He left the trio sitting in the room completely puzzled. So far, they didn't think Craig came up with anything to charge anyone with murder, and they were still in the dark as to the threats.

Craig had delved into the background of the suspects and had questioned others that Laura and Brad didn't know about. There was no point in getting their hopes up.

Five minutes later, Ed Langston came into the room and sat down.

"What? No lie detector test?"

Craig's eyes were cold as he stared at him. Ed's face was flushed and his eyes were pinned. The guy was on drugs. This interrogation, however, didn't deal with drug usage, although, he hoped to expose him as an addict later.

Right now, he wanted some answers. "Why would you need a lie detector? Do you intend to lie?"

Ed laughed. "You think I'm foolish enough to answer that question?"

When he'd answered the preliminary questions, Craig got down to business. "I understand that Professor Scofield refused to keep you as a piano student."

"That's right."

"Can you tell me why?"

"I can, but I don't know why I should."

That ruffled Craig's feathers, but he stayed calm. "Unless you want to spend the night as a guest of the city, I suggest you answer."

Ed sighed heavily. "Scofield was a fool. He thought he could rule the lives of everyone around him."

"Tell me, what kind of a student were you?"

"It is without a doubt that I was an excellent student."

In the next room, Charles, Laura and Brad looked at each other.

Charles whispered. "Would he be so stupid as to say the same words that were used on the threats?"

Their attention went back to the interrogation.

Craig hesitated, hoping the three in the next room caught the words, *It is with.* Circumstantial as they may be, it was a clue to Ed's involvement. "Yet your chosen profession has nothing to do with music."

"That's right. I teach English at the local high school."

"And is that rewarding?"

Ed nodded. "For the most part."

"Do they allow you to use drugs?"

Ed shot out of the chair and bent over the table. "Don't be like my uncle. You know nothing about nothing. Just what do you want from me?"

"Did you write threatening notes to Laura Westlund?"

"Why would I do that?"

"Why indeed? You don't seem shocked that she received threats."

He shrugged. "It's none of my business."

"I beg to differ with you. Were you out of town between May ninth and May twenty-first?"

He shook his head as he scowled.

"I'll be more specific. Where were you on Sunday, May ninth?"

"I suppose I was at home since it was on a Sunday. I usually stay in all day Sunday and catch up with work around the house. I'm also writing articles that I hope to have published. That's my only day to really dig into that work."

"How about Friday, May fourteenth?"

Ed contemplated. "Friday. Oh, yes. We had a debate at the school all day Friday and we entertained the winners that evening. I was at school all day and evening. You can check that."

"What about Thursday, May twentieth?"

"School as usual with play practice after school. Anything else?"

"I may get back to you with more questions. I hope you'll cooperate if I call you in again."

"It is with little pleasure that. . . never mind. Whatever you want."

"What were you going to say?"

"Unimportant."

Craig shrugged and said the testimony would be typed and brought back for his signature.

Meanwhile, Laura Charles and Brad all realized that Craig had heard those damaging words from Ed during their telephone conversation. That was why he left Ed for last.

"Can't Craig just arrest him now?"

Brad held up his hand. "That's pretty circumstantial evidence, not to mention he has alibis."

"*It is with* little something or other. Each of the notes started with that." Charles turned to Laura. "Is that what bothered you about him?"

"I don't know."

Brad was thoughtful. "I suppose there are others who use those words. It wouldn't hold up in court."

"I suppose not. Even Ed's uncle used those words." She looked down with a frown and then her head snapped back up. "That's it," she said excitedly. "That's what bothered me. Professor Standish used those words a lot when I took his class. We used to tease Ed about it. Every time we'd meet him in the hall, someone would say, 'Like uncle, like nephew.' It really bothered him. All he'd say to defend himself is that if a man as smart as his uncle used the expression, there wasn't anything wrong with it."

They looked at each other. "His uncle?"

Laura nodded. "Professor Allen Standish."

Craig entered the room. "Well? What do you think?"

They all spoke at the same time. "Professor Allen Standish."

After Laura explained, Craig agreed to question the professor. Craig called and learned that Professor Standish would be back late tonight. He said he would call him again in the morning.

"This gets worse, not better," complained Charles.

"That's what we deal with every day. Nothing makes sense. Nothing adds up until that light bulb comes on." He pointed to his head. "Then it all makes sense. Let's hold out for that."

That night, Charles and Laura walked around the campus, reminiscing. He wanted so badly to put his arm around her, but he was serious about getting this mess cleared up before delving into their relationship. Somehow, he felt there wouldn't be a problem. They had wasted six years of their lives. Now, they were given a second chance. He knew now that he didn't come back to the states purely by chance, nor was it coincidence that he learned of Laura's concert in Chicago. No, God had brought them together again.

They walked behind the auditorium on the path to the music building.

Laura shivered a little. "It's getting dark."

"And cold," said Charles as he put his arm around her shoulder and drew her closer. "Maybe we should get back to the car. May nights can be chilly."

She nodded, enjoying their closeness. "Let's go to the visual arts building. I want you to look at something through the window if the cleaning people are still there."

They got to the building. "There." She pointed. "Look inside."

He looked inside and couldn't believe his eyes. "My painting."

She nodded. "Your portrait of Professor Chalmers. He was your inspiration, and you were his."

"What do you mean?"

"He left the portrait here for future students to see, but he went to Italy to paint the scenes he had always wanted to paint. You showed him how to follow his dream, just as you followed yours."

"I don't know what to say. He didn't know that the only reason I went to Paris was to run away from you. Studying was the last thing on my mind." He turned to face her. "In spite of everything we went through, do you know how lucky we are?"

She nodded and moved closer to him. She buried her head in his shoulder, his face buried in her hair. It felt so right.

"How touching." The voice came from the shadow behind them. "Don't bother to turn around. I have a gun."

Laura stiffened and Charles held her close. "What do you want from us?"

The voice laughed. "You of course. God does work in mysterious ways. I was about to look for you at the hotel."

"Why?"

"No need for you to know that. We are going to get into your car. Charles, you will drive, both of you in the front seat." When they didn't move, he growled. "Now!"

She glanced at Charles. The man sounded like Professor Standish even if he didn't use outrageous words. Laura was beginning to panic. If he had been responsible for the notes, would he actually harm them? She'd remembered the pressure on her shoulder when her would-be abductor had her in a choke hold. The person who tried to abduct her was short . . . like Professor Standish.

Charles saw a look of recognition behind the fear in Laura's eyes. The man with a gun meant business. He could tell that much, and once he got them inside the car, all hope of escape would be gone.

Craig had contacted the clinic where Al Freeman had had day surgery. It turned out that he was there from five AM to a little after nine. That meant he had the opportunity to be by the police station at the same time Laura was there, but what was his motive? He'd have to call him back in.

It had been a long day and it was almost ten o'clock when he put on his jacket to leave. He had tried to call Professor Standish one more time and was told he was back in town, but was catching up with some work at the college tonight. Maybe he'd take a swing around there on his way home. He'd alerted his men in the squad cars to look out for a late model gold Toyota and . . . Craig suddenly remembered that it was a Toyota that the would-be abductor wanted Laura to get into. He hit the heel of his hand against his forehead.

He tried to call Laura, but was told she hadn't returned to the hotel. He got on the radio and told all squad cars to look out for the Toyota. He gave the license number and informed them that he was headed for the campus. If anything happened to Laura and Charles . . . He grabbed his keys and ran to his car. He used his flashing lights, but not the siren. Advertising his arrival would only chase him off, if indeed he was at the college.

The squad cars would go around the front, so he went around the back of the complex and passed the science building, then the music building. He frowned when he saw a car parked where it said NO PARKING. A closer look proved it to be a gold Toyota.

Charles had to think. He'd have to do something, but he wanted to know why they were being abducted.

"Just what is it you want?" he asked.

"Does it matter?"

"Of course." Laura stopped walking and turned around to face him. As frightened as she was, she stared him straight in the eye and spoke with a strong voice. "You tried to abduct me from the hotel parking lot. Why?"

"Isn't that obvious, my dear? I tried to warn you, but you wouldn't listen."

"You said you were going to get me. Why?"

"You were getting too close. I thought if I frightened you, you would leave."

"Too close to what?" asked Charles.

He sighed heavily. "I suppose there's no harm in telling you since you will not be able to enlighten anyone, unless, of course, you believe in angels."

"I happen to believe in God *and* angels," said Laura. She couldn't believe that God wouldn't help them now.

"Too bad. By the time anyone gets here to help you, it will be too late."

"Finish the story."

Professor Standish glared at Charles, but went on. "Why not? When Scofield found out about Eduardo's addiction, he was furious and banned him from his class. Not only that, but he threatened to tell the powers that be about my nephew, claiming that I condoned and enabled his behavior. You see, at that time, no one knew we were related. My sister Leona was furious. She had it all planned. Get Scofield drunk and threaten to contact the media. She thought he would reinstate Eduardo without an argument."

Charles narrowed his eyes. They were getting a little more than they bargained for. This had to do with Scofield. Had Standish killed him? If so, the only reason he was talking now was because he planned to kill them. *Keep him talking,* he told himself. *It's our only chance.* "I see. Then you decided that the college was better off without Scofield."

"Yes. No." He took a deep breath, and waved them forward with the gun. "No more talk. Get into the car."

As they approached the car, Charles winked at Laura, hoping she'd know that she should expect him to do something soon. They were at the passenger side. The professor pressed his key fob to unlock the door and motioned Charles to open the door. This was his only chance. He swung the door open quickly, his movements sure and fluid as his arm extended out beyond the door, catching Standish off guard and knocking the gun out of his hand. It all happened so fast, Laura barely had time to slip out of the way to kick the gun away. It was then that she noticed a police car driving by the front of the college.

If only she could get their attention.

Charles had the professor's arm twisted behind his back and none too gently. "Go on with your story."

He shook his head and winced with the pain that shot through his arm as Charles twisted it higher. He huffed, but relented. "I did as Leona said. I went over to see him."

Craig, who had been there for some time, got out of the car unnoticed and approached them from behind.

Charles put more pressure on his arm. "Go on."

Standish shook his head. "My life has been parsimonious, at best. It's ineffable--"

"Common English, Standish!" said Craig as he approached from behind them.

Standish glared at Craig. *Ignorant public servant!* He'd thought he could silence Laura and Templeton, but there was no hope of that now. His jaw tightened and he felt the pressure increase on his arm. "He said he'd taken a sleeping pill but still wasn't able to sleep. He was groggy and he looked terrible. I had brought a bottle of brandy with me and I told him in a most friendly manner that in order to really work, he must drink this potion. He said he didn't drink alcohol, but I told him that doctors have used this method for years. In his condition it didn't take long to convince him. He finally took a sip at a time until he'd finished the glass. He was feeling pretty good, so when he asked for more, I gave it to him. He couldn't have cared less when I snapped some pictures of him holding the bottle. He mumbled something about another pill. I gave him one and put the bottle on the table beside him and left. The next day I learned he was dead."

"Why were your finger prints not on the pill bottle?"

Standish shrugged. "I wiped them off."

Craig was thoughtful. "You wiped the prints off the bottle?"

"That is precisely what I said," he snapped.

"What is it?" whispered Laura.

"There were partial prints on the bottle, but nothing we could use."

Charles nodded. "Someone else was there after Standish left?"

Craig pondered that. "Had to be."

Another squad car pulled up.

After handcuffing him, Craig told the other officer to read him his rights and book him. "Did he intend to kill Scofield?" Laura and Charles shrugged. "Either way, I'll get it out of him. I'll go over the autopsy report. This whole thing will be cleared up once and for all. Then I can retire." The three of them watched as the patrol car drove off.

"Good work, Templeton. I'll need you two to come to the station to make a statement. Tomorrow's soon enough."

Laura narrowed her eyes. "Do you mean that you were waiting to solve the crime before you retired?"

Craig smiled. "In a way. The evidence pointed to suicide, but in my mind, it wasn't really solved. That was not a good time for the police chief to retire." He said goodnight and left.

It was eleven o'clock when Chares and Laura walked into the hotel lobby.

"What a night," she said.

When they were in the elevator, he took her hand. "I'm afraid you're going to find life dull after this."

She laughed. "I don't think I'll complain about *dull* for a while."

Once they were in the suite, he took her into his arms. "Maybe we can make life more interesting if we do it together."

"Hmmm. I always was an advocate of togetherness."

They walked into the police station the next morning, eager to get their statements taken and get on with their lives.

Craig came out of his office. "Come into my office when you get done," he said and went back in.

Later, Laura knocked on his door. "You wanted to see us?"

Craig was smiling. "Come in, come in."

They sat down and waited to hear what he had to say.

"I think I've solved the whole thing. Coffee?" When they declined, he went on. "Carol Harding was the one who made it impossible for you to cancel Webster City because she had a need to tell you off in person. You already know that Al Freeman acted purely out of loyalty to Carol Harding. He thought by delivering that one note, he would scare you enough to leave. When that didn't work, he happened to see you get out of the car by the station. He was on his way home from his day surgery. He'd intended only to scare you."

He checked his notes. "Stu Engleman and Ed Langston had no part in any of this except their antagonism toward Scofield. Cindy Meyer's only crime was to plagiarize your musical. You can get a lawyer and take action against her. Professor Standish did the rest."

"But what was his motive?"

"As far as I can tell, Scofield threatened to expose him to the College Board. He was in denial as to Ed's using drugs. He was scared of his sister's reaction. They must have had some childhood. He was actually frightened into doing what she told him to do." He closed the file. "So there you have it. All is well that ends well."

"What will they do the Professor Standish?"

"That's up to a jury. If they believe he didn't mean to kill Scofield, he might get off with manslaughter. If they determine that Scofield took more of the sleeping pills on his own," he shrugged, "he still stands to get some of the blame."

Laura was troubled. "But if Fredrick didn't touch alcohol, how could he do a complete about face and do what Professor Standish asked of him?"

"Have you ever taken a sleeping pill?"

"Only once when I was in the hospital. Never again. I started to get out of bed so my roommate called for a nurse. I didn't even know it."

Craig smiled and waited for her to realize what she was saying. "He was already under the influence of sleeping pills. People do strange things when their minds aren't working right."

They stood up to leave. "Thank you for everything." Laura hugged him and planted a kiss on his cheek and Charles shook his hand.

"And what happens now with you two?"

They looked at each other. "We wondered," said Charles grinning, "if you would like to give the bride away."

Craig broke out in a jovial laugh. "I was hoping you two would wise up. When?"

Laura laughed, "We don't know yet. We just decided last night. I'd be so honored if you would walk me down the aisle."

"I'm the one who is honored, Laura."

They left like a couple of giggling kids. "I told you so," said Charles.

"I know. I'm so glad you suggested it. He really was more like my father than my father was. Let's go home and make some plans."

"One stop first."

"Where?"

"The jeweler. I want to buy you the ring I couldn't afford six years ago. I'm putting a claim on you for all to see." He kissed her forehead. "Life is going to be great no matter where we are."

"She nodded. "As long as we're together."

A week later, Craig called Laura in Chicago. "I have some news."

"About the homicide?"

"Yes. After you left, I thought I'd try to bluff Standish and I told him we had partial prints on the bottle. I said I'd compared the partial prints against his and . . . Well, I actually did compare them and they were very different."

Laura had put the phone on speaker. She glanced at Charles. "That means that he didn't go there with murder on his mind."

"Right. He'll be up for manslaughter."

"In a way, I feel sorry for him. It was all his sister's doing."

Charles looked through squinted eyes. "The man didn't have to do as his sister told him."

"True."

"Who gave him the rest of the pills?"

Craig hesitated. "The most obvious person."

Laura and Charles frowned with confusion. "Who?

"Scofield himself. I compared the partial prints with the prints of everyone involved. We didn't do it before because a partial print couldn't be presented as evidence. That small part of the fingerprint might match those of hundreds of people. Now that we know to what extent Standish was involved, we can assume the rest. Just to be on the safe side, I compared the prints to those of all of our suspects. No contest. They didn't match any of them. With Scofield's prints, they're too close to ignore. It had to be him. For what reason, we'll never know unless he did it in a drunken stupor. Don't worry. It will all work out." Craig was relieved that the whole thing was over, except for the trial. Somehow, he had a feeling that the jury would sympathize with Standish. He may pay a price, but he might avoid a long prison sentence. Time would tell.

"What about Alvin and Carol?"

"Are you sure you don't want to press charges?"

Laura hesitated. "I'd like them to be scared that I will. I don't want them to do anything like this again."

"And Cynthia Meyer? I put a good scare into her."

"Let's leave it that way. I don't want to hurt the college, but I'm not so sure I should just forget about the musical. I'll think of something."

"Now," said Craig, "tell me about the wedding."

"Well, it will be in a month or two. We have yet to work out the details, but it won't be long. Neither one of us wants a long engagement."

Charles chuckled. "I'd say six years is long enough. After all, we were still engaged. Weren't we?"

"I guess we were."

"Just let me know where and when. Lydia and I will be there with bells on."

Epilogue

Charles was standing by the altar, nervously waiting for Laura to walk down the aisle. Why was he nervous? Nothing could happen now, could it? Not in a million years did he dream that he and Laura would finally be married. Six years of their lives were wasted with bitterness, depression and self pity. Were those years truly wasted? He didn't think so. Yes, they were brokenhearted and lonely, but they were years in which he had grown, years in which he had become not only a man, but had made a name for himself. He was recognized in Europe and America for his exquisite French scenes. His goal now was to teach and spend his spare time painting the scenery of the United States. Until he'd made that decision, he hadn't realized that he'd been homesick for six long years. His stubbornness had gotten him through the first year. After that, life became a habit. Now life would begin again with Laura. He glanced up as the organ played the Bridal March. His heart skipped a beat. *She's even more beautiful now than she was then. I have to be the luckiest man alive to be waiting here for my beautiful bride. And I will paint her in her beautiful white wedding gown.*

Was this really happening? Craig held out his arm, ready to escort Laura down the aisle. As they took each step, she wanted to run to Charles for fear that something would happen to prevent the ceremony from becoming reality. No. Nothing could happen now. She could feel it. God brought them together. God would keep them together. She took a deep breath and smiled at Craig.

"Just a few more steps," whispered Craig and he returned her smile.

They had chosen the chapel at the college for the wedding. It seemed fitting since both she and Charles would be teaching there next year. They had one month for their honeymoon, which they intended to spend at Lake Vermilion in northern Minnesota. Charles rented a cabin on the south side of the lake. He and Laura would spend some of their honeymoon taking in the spectacular scenery, that is, if they had any spare time. They were still getting to know each other, but neither of them needed rose colored glasses to see a bright future for them

Brad stood up a little straighter. Charles had asked him to be their best man. He was honored, and looking at the Maid of Honor, he thought Melissa McAllister was very nice looking, and closer to his age than Laura. Besides, he never did hope he and Laura could become a couple, not really. He glanced from Charles to Laura. He could see the love in their eyes. Maybe there was hope for him. As Melissa came to stand by him, he winked at her. Was she blushing? Darned if she wasn't.

Craig kissed Laura's cheek and gave her hand to Charles before making his way to sit beside Lydia. A fitting end to a very long six years. He took his wife's hand in his as they witnessed the short ceremony.

There were only a few close friends at the wedding. There would be a reception when they returned from their honeymoon which included fellow artists and people from both of their careers. Charles assured her that none of his peers from Paris would attend, except for his beloved teacher. Wild horses couldn't keep him away. He had to meet the woman who had once broken the heart of his student.

"I present to you Mr. and Mrs. Charles Templeton."

A new name and a new life, thought Laura as she looked into her husband's eyes. Life was indeed wonderful.